So
for real

REBEKAH WEATHERSPOON

Books by Rebekah

VAMPIRE SORORITY SISTERS
Better Off Red
Blacker Than Blue
Soul to Keep

STAND ALONES
The Fling
At Her Feet
Treasure

THE FIT TRILOGY
Fit
Tamed
Sated

SUGAR BABY NOVELLAS
So Sweet
So Right
So For Real

Praise for Rebekah's work

"There are actually more really great romance authors out there, but it's only every now and then that you come across writing that makes you say, "This author is going places." Rebekah Weatherspoon is one of those authors." - Pandora Esperanza, *The Last Word Book Reviews*

AT HER FEET

"Indeed, the more I read *At Her Feet* I came to realize that it is the best and most original book that I have read in any genre for a very long time." – Jim Lyon, *The Seattle PI*

FIT

"I felt satisfied by a complete story at the end, and would highly recommend this to anyone looking for a fun, relatable contemporary romance." - Elisa Verna, *Romantic Times Book Reviews (TOP PICK REVIEW)*

TAMED

"The second in Weatherspoon's Fit series, "Tamed" is another must-read for fans of BDSM romance. - Elisa Verna, *Romantic Times Book Reviews (TOP PICK REVIEW)*

TREASURE

"This story is rich yet beguiling, magnificent yet down to earth, and intriguing yet heartwarmingly human." – J.J., *Rainbow Book Reviews*

Acknowledgement

Thank you to the twin moms, VN, JL, E, EB, AB, JB, who educated and scared the living crap out of me in one conversation.

XO to you and your tiny humans. x2.

Dedication

To Mr. and Mrs. Bradbury

Chapter One

I learned a lot about myself while I was planning our wedding. I learned a whole lot about my family. Like how my little sisters, Kaleigh and Kiara, were willing to actually murder each other for the title of Maid of Honor. I also learned that my mother was completely prepared to disown me if I thought for one second that my fiancé, Michael, and I were going to exchange vows anywhere other than an actual church.

I learned that marrying an actual billionaire came with some interesting perks and requests, like having your engagement photos in the Times and your wedding photos exclusively featured in the most popular women's magazine in the country.

I learned that when you had a best friend like Daniella, she was the right choice for Maid of Honor because she actually made the best go-between with my overzealous aunts and my butt hurt roommates from college, who I literally hadn't spoken to in five years, but invited anyway. I learned that Daniella was really awesome at making lists and delegating tasks and deflecting nonsense, and I had to keep her as my best friend forever and buy her an expensive exotic animal or a boat. Michael and I would have eloped without her.

There was an amazing engagement party. Two actually—marrying rich was weird. A fun as hell bachelorette party and the best bridal shower a girl could ask for. So many details I'd never considered, but when the day came, I could only think of one thing: I was marrying Michael Bradbury. The way we met, at a Sugar baby/Sugar Daddy cocktail party two summers before, both awkward and uncomfortable and completely out of our elements. What we both wanted and how we each ended up being exactly what the other needed. I never could have imagined it this way. Never in a million years.

Our engagement had lasted a little over a year. My mother had a guest list to review and opinions on flowers and accessories, and this was her first baby walking down the aisle. She would not be rushed. In that year, I became more and more secure in the fact that Michael was the perfect man for me. His ridiculously good looks aside, even when I tried looking, there was no flaw to be found, or maybe our flaws just meshed so perfectly.

Michael opened up more, letting his guard down, letting me be my true self. I don't know when it happened or how, but suddenly he was my person, the one I could tell anything and everything, the one I consulted first, and even though he tried to spare me the details of his business deals, he started to really turn to me when he was undecided or just needed to vent. He knew he could tell me when his mother's deteriorating health was eating him up inside, how sometimes he felt like the shittiest brother and the shittiest absentee uncle because sometimes he could only send gifts and money when his job made a pitstop to the midwest impossible.

We built a trust, something I'd never experienced with anyone else before. He was mine and I was his, lover and best friend, my soulmate, the filling in my heart pie, and we got to kick it together until death do us part. I couldn't wait to spend the rest of our lives together. I was fucking excited just to start.

Our wedding week was a blur. Once we arrived in Michigan, it felt like a race to some sort of bizarre finish line and luckily we made it, incident free. Everyone showed up, everyone looked great. No special vows, just the word the church had to offer, by the book, but I was feeling a tad sentimental so I tasked my cousin, Julianne, with noting the exact time the Reverend pronounced us husband and wife. It was five thirty-four p.m. I told her to write it down and email it to me, too. I didn't want there to be any chance that I would forget.

It took everyone a little while to make their way out of the church. We waited with our wedding party as our photographer, Shannon, got us situated on the elaborate steps that wrapped around St. Andrew's Episcopal. She had a plan that involved a particular set of birch-encased windows. I grabbed Michael's hand and held it to the side of my neck. I'd been a mix of happy and nervous for the last few months, but nothing prepared me for just how excited I'd be once I became a Mrs.

"Can you feel that?"

I knew he could. My pulse was actually pounding.

"I can." He kissed me again quickly on the lips, then smiled. "Don't pass out on me, okay?"

"I promise I won't. Are you okay?"

I couldn't stop looking at him. Everything else around us was moving in high speed, but all I could see was him. Michael was standing there in front of me on the church's brick steps in stark high def, slow motion. His color was way up and his eyes were still a little watery. I knew he was going through his own range of emotions, but he was my husband now. Checking on his general welfare was my duty.

"You look like you sniffed some real good shit," I teased, then kissed him again.

"I don't think I can explain how more than okay I am right now. I love you."

"I love you." I leaned up on my toes and kissed him some more. When he pulled away just a little, I realized our whole wedding party was perfectly positioned around us and Shannon had already started snapping away. We took a million more pictures while Zia, my new friend and traveling makeup artist, and Malika, our wedding planner, directed our guests over to the Paultin Conservatory for the reception.

Laughing at the jokes Michael's friend Duke and Daniella's sister Lili would not stop cracking during our photo session helped calm my nerves and level me out a bit, but I was still plenty flustered when Michael and I finally climbed into our private car. Finally, it was just the two of us. I turned to my husband, but before I could get a word out he pulled me into his lap and started hiking up the miles and miles of flowy fabric I was wearing.

I had picked the dress for comfort and ease over style, but the lace and chiffon were still gorgeous. A little revealing up top, with a plunging neckline. I figured we'd be so busy with smiling and thanking people and making small talk that Michael wouldn't even get the opportunity to look under the hood until we got to our honeymoon suite much, much later that night. Holy shit, was I wrong.

"What are you doing?" His lips on my neck made it a little hard to breathe again.

His hand slipped roughly up my thigh. I spread my legs and arched toward his searching fingers, even though I knew we shouldn't. The Conservatory wasn't that far away.

"You're not wearing that spanx thing, are you?" Before I could even answer, his hand was groping my crotch. He already had his answer. Again, the day was about comfort. Full body, inch thick, tighter-than-skin spandex spelled anything but comfort to me. I'd opted for a pair of lace panties that offered a hint of sexiness while providing the butt coverage needed to keep the fabric from riding clean up my ass while I tried to out Cha Cha Slide my sisters during the reception.

Michael pulled the lace aside and gently fondled my suddenly swollen lips. It only took a few strokes before I was soaking wet. He slid a finger inside me and then pulled it out again, once and then again before his fingers moved over my clit.

"No. Oh god, babe. We have to get over to the reception," I said. The car was still idling at the curb.

"No, the fuck we don't. Not yet."

"But we have to do the...the whole grand entrance." I bit down on my smudge proof lip tint to smother a desperate moan. His erection was pressing against my ass, through the fabric of his suit. We were still technically in the middle of our wedding and we had people waiting for us.

"Michael—" He silenced me with another deep kiss before he pulled back and looked me in the eye.

"Kayla. Baby. Relax. I talked to Zia. I talked to Daniella who is gonna talk to Malika. I talked to my sister. I talked to the driver. I just want one minute with my wife. There is booze and entertainment. There is plenty to keep everyone busy. Please—" I gasped as two fingers pushed deep inside of my pussy. "Let me enjoy the first few minutes of married life with my wife."

Okay, what he was saying was nice, but the way he smiled, so smug, so satisfied, so happy when he said the words "my wife," all while stroking me in the most dirty of ways...I almost came on his hand right then.

"Well," I groaned as I wrapped my arm around his shoulder to help steady myself on his lap. "I think you're right. I'm sorry. I'm still in responsible bride mode. I want more than a few minutes alone with you, too." I'd been so focused on blowing his mind during our honeymoon, I'd put the option of quality pants-off time out of my mind until then. But part of me had forgotten who I was dealing with. This was

Michael Bradbury, and with him, as long as you didn't violate any law of public indecency, any time was pants-off time. I shifted closer, spreading my legs even wider until my knees were hooked on either side of his thighs.

"Have I mentioned that I love you?"

"I—" I couldn't speak. Michael had my clit gently between his fingers. I was going to come any second. My hip swirled against his hand, my aching muscles desperate for more. A strong orgasm tackled my senses, forcing me to press my forehead against Michael's as I shuddered through the pleasure. "I love you too," I whimpered.

Michael's lips found mine again, his kisses probably the best and worst thing to help me come down. His cock was still hard against my leg when I could finally see straight. I kept on kissing him, but slid off his lap and went right for his belt. I was so glad he'd decided on a simple suit and not a tux with a ton of unnecessary pieces like a cummberbund or a vest. His erection practically popped into my hand as he wiggled his pants and boxer briefs out of the way. His dick was hard and thick, enough to fill one hand and long enough to stroke with two. I gripped him firm, feeling him up and down as I watched the satisfied look on his face.

"Don't fuck up my hair," I instructed him with a deadly glare before I leaned over his lap. "I mean it."

"I won't, baby." His laugh turned into a groan. Zia finished my makeup off with some type of outdoor deck sealant so my wedding day face isn't going anywhere, blow job or no, but my hair was another matter. It would have been obvious if Michael had gotten a desperate handful. As I traced the head of his cock a few times with my tongue, he followed my strict orders, toying with the row of pearl buttons running down the deceptively sheer fabrics covering my back.

I rushed. I knew I did. No matter what he told who, my mom raised a good southern girl and at the very least she would say it was rude to keep that many people waiting too long. Especially when Michael and I had ten days of no-pants time and butt stuff just around the corner. I sucked him deep and hard, and stroked him the desperate way he liked when we both got a little rough and carried away. I did the one thing I knew would drive him crazy—I looked him in the eye while I was jerking him. I saw the tension spread across his forehead and his fingers spread wide on my back. He knew better than to pop one of my buttons. He refused to close his eyes when he came. They narrowed to small slits as he cursed and groaned my name, filling my mouth with every drop he had.

He had clearly thought of everything 'cause there was a festively decorated basket in one of the jump seats. I didn't notice it at first, but Michael handed me some water and mints, then cleaned himself up with some wet wipes. There was lotion, something I'd made a serious part of his life, and when we were all fresh and tidy—my hair still perfectly in place—Michael cracked the door and told the driver we were ready to go.

He settled back in the seat next to me and took my hand, brushing his lips against my knuckles before he kissed the back of my hand. I was still a little high from my orgasm but those small, sweet gestures made me want to cry all the tears that hadn't escaped during our simple vows.

"Is this what married life is going to be like with you, Mr. Bradbury?" I teased.

"Mrs. Bradbury," he said before he kissed me on the temple. "This life will be whatever you want it to be. Just tell me and it's yours."

The billions lining his bank account made that statement absolutely doable, but I believed him because I knew he loved me just that much.

Yeah, yeah saying our vows was great and shit, but I think Michael and I had the best reception in the history of wedding receptions. The food was delicious and plentiful, a fancy spin on southern barbecue with gluten free and vegetarian options. DJ Makeway took a break from his world tour to spin and emcee. Michael and I shared our first dance to a new favorite off De'bonay's most recent album. Of course she was there to sing it for us live. Kiara and Kaleigh, and Myra and Matthew made the most adorable toasts and I couldn't help but weep like a baby because my heart was full to bursting. I knew how lucky Michael and I were. We both had great families and now the number of sweet, caring people in our lives had officially doubled.

I danced with my dad to some mix he'd rigged up with the DJ, a combo of Stevie Wonder's "Isn't She Lovely" and Prince's "1999," both bathtime favorites when I was a kid. Michael's mom Nina still struggled in her ongoing battle with dementia, but she was in great spirits and let Michael twirl her around the dance floor to a James Taylor classic. After that I made a pact with Michael because we've been to enough social functions together. No separating. We worked the room together, hand in hand greeting our families and friends. Team Bradbury FTW. We skipped cutting a cake because it was such a weird tradition to me and Michael wasn't too hung up on it either and instead treated our guests to a sweets bar with all the mini cupcakes and brownies and tarts they could handle.

I fought against it at first, but Michael's business partner and his wife, insisted on arranging a gifting suite for our guests. I mean there are goodie bags and then there are bags with nearly fifteen thousand dollars worth of free shit, but when my fifteen-year-old cousin came running up to me, losing his shit because he never thought he'd have a smartwatch, I remembered again that having money was not a bad thing. As the night stretched on, Michael and I made a stealth exit. We had plans for brunch with our families and whichever guests decided to hang around the following morning, but finally it was *US* time.

We'd already been in Michigan for a little over a week, staying at a large rental with Holger, our primary housekeeper, and our dogs Patch and Penny, but that night we checked into this adorable honeymoon suite at a local hotel Michael's sister had picked out for us. Daniella and my mom told me a hundred times that they would take care of everything and Ruben, Michael's personal assistant, teamed with Holger to make sure all of our clothes and personal odds and ends were there waiting for us. There were other surprises waiting when we opened the honeymoon suite door.

Michael stepped behind me and immediately started unbuttoning my dress. I shivered as his lips traced over my bare shoulder. I was exhausted and champagne drunk, but this was a moment I'd been waiting for for over a year. Making love to my husband.

"I have strict instructions," he whispered against my skin as he gently gripped the fabric that had pooled around my waist and pushed it down to the floor.

"From who?" I covered my boobs, doing my best to spare Michael from the boob lift tape pads we had to rig up so I could wear my dress without a bra.

"Daniella."

"And what were her instructions?"

"To treat you like the most precious thing in my world."

"Is that so?"

"It is. If you'll follow me." Michael took my hand, laughing a bit as I was forced to reveal the horrible price my tits had paid for fashion. We walked through the main sitting room, into the bedroom and then further into the massive bathroom. I glanced back at the bedroom. There were candles lit and rose petals everywhere. It looked so nice.

"Where are we going?" I asked impatiently. "The bed is right here. Let's have sex on the bed."

"And we will, I promise." Michael smiled that half smile this time. He was humoring me. I turned back and saw what he was getting at. Lit candles and rose petals in the bathroom too. There were two plush bath robes hanging on a hook outside the huge walk-in shower and all sorts of toiletries arranged on the vanity counters. Michael gently helped me pull the breast form thingies off my boobs and then he pulled my underwear down. I stepped out of them and walked into the big fluffy towel Michael was holding open for me. I secured it around my chest and looked up at him.

"We're halfway there. Now you just take off your pants at least and we can make this man and wife shit real official."

"On the counter, please, if you will."

I shook my head at him, but shuffled up on the sturdy marble surface. Michael made a show of slowly removing his suit jacket and then his tie.

"We're gonna see if I'm any good at this."

"At what??" I laughed.

He ignored me and grabbed a little folded card hidden among the toiletries, then started searching like he was about to bake a cake. When he turned back to me, he was holding a small cloth and a really expensive bottle of makeup remover.

"If you'll close your eyes please. We can begin."

I did what he asked but I still laughed at him a little. "Babe, this is the weirdest foreplay. I could have taken off my own makeup."

"I was talking to Daniella and Zia about how much I love you and Zia mentioned that if I really loved you, I'd make sure that you didn't fall asleep with all this stuff on." I nodded as he went on. I usually liked to scrub off a layer of my face when I was getting ready for bed at night, but he was being so gentle. "I thought about our usual nightly rituals and the pact we'd made and how for the next two weeks I have no reason to leave your side."

My eyes popped open and I looked up at him. I thought my chest was going to cave in.

"I knew I would either forget or get caught up in trying to dick you down something special because it's our wedding night, damn right I have something to prove and then you'd wake up, and—"

"I'd roll out of bed groaning and complaining about how gross my face feels and you'd feel extra guilty for not reminding me?"

"Exactly. When we get back—"

"Don't say it," I said throwing my head back dramatically, which was a big mistake because I was still pretty tipsy.

"Okay, I won't. But we both know."

"So you help me take off my makeup and tomorrow I help you shave and we're one of those married couples who make people want to barf."

"We're a husband and wife who actually love each other. I married you because I want to be with you. Always. But since *always* isn't exactly possible, I'll have to settle for as often as possible."

I was too choked up to say anything sweet or even witty back so I just nodded and closed my eyes again, letting a few fat tears of joy run down my face as he finished the job.

And then he took the forty-eight pins out of my half updo and let me undress him. We showered together, kissing and caressing, teasing each other until we couldn't take it anymore.

He was hard, erection standing at attention as he led me back into the bedroom. More champagne, a private toast to our future, to us. There was something really hot about watching my husband partake in the bubbly while standing in front of me, butt naked. I told him as much and that seemed to be the end of his patience. Michael and I finally made love. We'd had sex the day before, but this time it was married sex and it was freaking amazing.

After, he dug up my silk scarf and lay beside me stroking my side and thigh as I preserved the super expensive eighteen inch bundles I'd bought just for the occasion. When he finally cut off the lights it was technically a new day, but I still wanted to include those couple of hours past midnight, those precious minutes, as part of the best day of my life.

Chapter Two

Here's the thing about traveling to Europe. It doesn't matter how excited you are to go, you feel like roadkill when you get there. People had warned me. Michael's personal assistant, Ruben, had been to Europe a ton of times with his boyfriend. He definitely warned me and other people, well other people mentioned it too when they found out where Michael and I were spending our honeymoon, but most people were really shocked when I told them I'd never been to Europe before. When you date a man like Michael, apparently you're supposed to circumnavigate the globe for fun on the weekends, but Michael and I had both been really busy since we met. Even though we knew it was going to take up a lot of his time, his ownership of a professional basketball team took up time he didn't even have.

We had our weekend breaks here and there, and proper holidays to see our families, but our honeymoon was our first real big trip together. I was in and out on the plane, but I was too anxious to really sleep. Michael had the sleep habits of a PhD student on crank. He slept a little on the fifteen hour flight, but almost every time I woke up he was awake, answering some pre-vacay work emails or reading.

And as soon as we arrived at the refurbished shooting lodge (I thought it was a castle, but whatevs) on Loch Torridon on the west coast of Scotland, I was straining to keep my eyes open so we could take in the rustic luxury of it all. There was some gloppity gloop about staying awake until that evening so we could get on Scotland time, but that wasn't happening. We checked in, Michael ordered us some room service to pick at and then it was right to the room for some much needed rest and sexy times.

We'd booked this massive three room suite with a giant bathroom and a walk-out patio that overlooked the water. I was shocked by the bright, modern decor and I was sure I would enjoy the view after I caught that nap, which we did as soon as our bags were delivered to the room.

I was tempted to sleep the whole day away. They never tell you how much a wedding will kick your ass. Combine that with some international travel and it was lights out for Kaykay. Still, I woke up around one that afternoon and found my hot babe of a husband already showered and dressed. He was sitting in the armchair opposite the bed with his tablet, looking relaxed and oddly sophisticated. I needed to get him a fancy chair like that for his office. Or one of our bedrooms at home.

I smiled at him through my sleepy haze. My husband looked so good with his hair all damp and pulled back in a ponytail. As soon as he realized I was checking him out, he came back across the bedroom and kissed me on my cheeks.

"Hi," I whispered.

"Hello. So, hey, I know it's tempting to stay in this bed all day—"

"It is. We have to find out where they got this mattress from."

"I'm on top of it. But before we start furniture shopping, I have a little surprise for you. You up for a short walk?"

"Awww. Walk?" I said immediately pouting.

"Too much?" He laughed.

"No, no. Thinking about walks makes me miss the puppies." We tried to take Penny and Patch everywhere with us, but they had to sit this trip out.

"Don't worry. Holger already sent pictures. What do you say?"

"I say let me brush my teeth for the first time in a full twenty-four hours and you have yourself a deal, buddy." I slid out of bed and started backing toward the bathroom.

"Sounds great."

"You want an open-mouthed kiss first? I had some really good cheese on the plane yesterday while you were napping."

"You had to be gross about it. Now I don't want to kiss you."

"You sure?"

He just smiled at me again, shaking his head. I was sure he didn't regret marrying me at all.

Once I ungrossed myself, I followed Michael downstairs. As we walked by the front desk we were instructed to "Follow this hall right here to your left, and Innes and Gregory will be waiting for you." Sure enough, a tall pleasant woman with brown hair and a bright smile, and a scary looking dude with no hair, were waiting for us at the end of the corridor. They called me Mrs. Bradbury. It felt good.

Innes introduced herself. She'd be assisting us that afternoon and ole pissy-faced Greg was coming along to ensure our privacy. Aka safety.

Before Michael purchased The Flames, his official security team numbered exactly two. I had no clue 'cause he insisted on not drawing attention to himself, but his driver PJ was actually an ex-cop and Holger was ex-military, and both were strapped, eyes peeled at all times. Even our part-time housekeeper, Vera, had served on a police force in Romania before she came to the US. They blended in so well with our family and Michael's business that I never assumed a thing, but the minute Michael's hotness went viral, it was clear that we needed to step things up a bit.

Through PJ's contacts, John and Emmanuel had joined our little crew, making themselves a tad more conspicuous just in case anyone got any ideas. Nothing had happened, but Michael was actually stopped on the street now. He was really popular within the whole of the NBA, with players and fans, because of how down to Earth and involved with the team he was, and after one visit to a top-rated late night show it was a wrap. People who had just seen pictures of him got to hear how sexy his voice was and you know how that goes. And his friendship with Duke, De'Bonay and the Chrises had made him more appealing. Paparazzi followed us, and by us I mean him, on a semi-regular basis. I was sure we'd kept our honeymoon location a secret, but in any case, Gregory was our man.

I took Michael's hand as we emerged from a side entrance of the magic castle and followed Innes down a beautiful wooded path. The cool air was a nice break from the August heat back home. She told us a bit about the property, knowing exactly how much to say to keep us interested without talking our heads off. She was quiet though as the woods broke, revealing a large grassy field. Two poshly dressed servers were standing on either side of a large plaid blanket, covered with an elaborate picnic lunch. There were a few neatly wrapped boxes among the flowers and china settings. That husband of mine had brought gifts.

"Was this worth the walk?" Michael teased, giving the back of my neck a gentle squeeze.

"No. This is awful. I want a divorce." I looked up at him. We'd just gotten to Scotland. I didn't need to start sobbing already. I could tell he could read my mind 'cause he leaned down and took me by the chin, softly kissed me on the lips.

We made ourselves comfortable and Innes explained what all four courses would entail. I won't lie and say Michael and I hadn't been out for our share of fancy dinners in the last year, but those were mostly business related. When it was just the two of us, Holger usually cooked our favorites or we ordered the most unhealthy takeout 'cause I am fat and

Michael's nearly a senior citizen. What did we have to lose?

The food was delicious, but it was honestly outdone by the setting and the company. After we finished the first course, Michael handed me a smallish square box wrapped in glossy white paper with a blue ribbon.

"We already exchanged wedding gifts," I said, opening the present anyway. Who doesn't like things? I'd gotten Michael this beautiful handmade pocket watch, then had another dirty haiku about how horny he made me engraved inside. It was not meant to be a family heirloom. He'd bought me a new car to match the one he'd recently upgraded to. I wanted to choke him, but when I opened the driver's side door I found a journal full of a year's worth of love notes he'd written for me starting from the day we began officially planning our wedding, I decided I could live with an SUV that cost almost as much as my parents' house. He'd even given his own poetry a try too. It was terrible and cute and so funny. My favorite among them:

> **Rose are red**
> **Violets are blue**
> **I considered getting a prescription to viagra today, but I figured an eight-hour erection wasn't worth the risk of dying on top of you from a heart attack or stroke.**
>
> **I love you.**

A car was plenty. The love notes were priceless. And I had Michael. I didn't need a single thing.

"I realized I don't spoil you enough," he said with a little smile. He was being bashful, but he was serious.

"Uh, what?"

"Open it."

"Here, put this in my hair. You can tie a bow, right?" I handed Michael the ribbon and turned my back to him.

"I think I can manage it." He scooped my hair off my shoulders and went to work.

When I pulled back the white paper, it revealed the engraved lid of a fancy jewelry store in Miami. Inside was this really cool multi-strand charm bracelet. Two different strings of pearls were interwoven with two strings of blue sapphires. The charms were all clustered near the clasp: a K and an M encrusted with diamonds, a large pearl heart and two small doggie charms. It was so beautiful and so me.

"Babe, I love this so much." I turned to face him. "Tell Gregory to avert his eyes."

"He's not looking."

"Okay good." I put down the bracelet and kissed Michael something good. It was one of those kisses that came just shy of a full blown make out session, but I came back to my senses and remembered we had an audience.

After the second course, Michael handed me a bigger box, same white wrapping with a more elaborate box. I was tempted to shake it in jest, but knowing my luck it would be a delicate crystal figurine. It was a figurine of sorts, alright. It was a red dildo laying on a delicately arranged white pillow.

"Okay. Tell me Gregory isn't looking for real this time."

"Trust me, baby. Gregory does not give a shit."

"Can I hold it?" I said, letting out the most unladylike snort.

"It's yours. You can do whatever you want with it."

"Don't make promises you can't keep, 'cause I'll ask Innes to run down to the village shop for a strap on and we can have some real fun."

I grabbed the dildo, weighing it in my hands and that was the exact moment one of the servers realized my water was low. Angela came over just in time to get a real good look at my new toy. She blushed purple and failed to hide her smile, but she kept it professional. Michael thanked her, drawing her attention away from the giant red cock in my hands. There was something about that cock. I just couldn't put my finger on it.

"Babe," I whispered. "This dick looks familiar." I whipped my head up as soon as I realized. "You didn't." I'd seen those Make-A-Dick kits, but this looked far more legit. It was an exact replica of his penis, cast in high-quality silicone. No seams, no odd bumps or bubbles. That dildo would outlive us both. "This is the real deal."

Michael shrugged. "It was an experience having to hold an erection while I had my dick 3D scanned, but you said you wanted me to take you both ways. I figure it's time we test it out."

"This will go nicely with the surprise I have for you tonight."

"Oh yeah?"

"Yes, but it's a surprise and, no, you'd don't get any hints."

After the third course, another smaller box, this time diamond earrings floating in a hexagonal setting that matched my engagement ring. That earned him another long, thorough kiss. He gave me my final gift—of the afternoon. He was sure to mention that—as we were enjoying our dessert. A framed picture of us standing at the altar. I closed my eyes for just a second, reliving the moment all over again.

"Of course you can put it wherever you like, but I figured it would look good in your office in the Miami house," he said, smiling wide. He knew he did good.

"How did you even manage this? It was like forty-eight hours ago and we've been traveling for half of that."

"I paid Shannon a little extra for a rush print job. Little hand off to Holger and it made it into my luggage."

"Well tell Shannon I said nice work." I stared at the picture for a few long moments, running my finger over the glass. Michael didn't say anything, just held me as I tried to wrangle my composure that was dangerously close to slipping. I realized this had been a consistent theme to our whole relationship and it would probably carry on throughout our marriage. I could be as silly and sarcastic as I wanted with Michael. He seemed to prefer it that way, but then he would blindside me with the most intense feelings of pure love.

I ran my finger over the two of us, looked at the way I was looking at him and the way he was looking at me and suddenly I wondered if it was too much for me to contain. And then I remembered I didn't have to.

Gently, I set the picture back down on top of the wrapping paper, then moved to my knees so I could turn around and face Michael.

"I'm not gonna say I don't deserve you 'cause I do. I'm fabulous."

He smiled and reached up to wiped a few renegade tears off my cheeks. "You are pretty great."

"Thank you. I do want to say I love you though, and I'm gonna have to give some of these feelings to you because I'm about to explode."

"Come here."

Michael wrapped his arms around me and pulled me down on the blanket, rolling so I was kind of under him. We missed the edge by an inch or so. I knew I'd have grass in my hair after, but that was just something I had to charge to the game. He looked at me closely, drawing his fingers lightly down my cheek. I looked at his deep blue eyes and then his lips as his hand made its way down my body, over the curve of my breast and farther down to my hip. He pulled me closer, rolling my body toward him as he kissed me soft and slow. Loving him for the rest of my life was gonna be a breeze.

We finished up our fancy picnic, then Gregory chaperoned a nice walk around part of the property while Innes assured us they would get all of our things, i.e. my gifts, up to the room. After our walk, we took another nap and then Michael arranged for a private dinner for us down in the larger of the castle's two libraries. Seriously, I didn't know on what planet you would call a place like this huge ass mansion complete with towers and everything a hunting lodge and not a castle, but I was sticking hard to this castle thing. Anyway, we got dressed up all nice and pretty, and headed down for another delicious meal.

The owners stopped in to greet us just before the first course was served, a really nice husband and wife who had recently taken over the place from her parents. Michael, of course, charmed them stupid. I'm sure they were just glad that the man they were making all these special accommodations for wasn't a complete dick. They told us more about the activities they offered guests, with the explicit reminder that any and all of the excursions, hikes, nature walks and trips to the shooting range can be made private at our request. I may have gasped and grabbed Michael's hand when they told us about their archery range. I didn't feel comfortable wielding a shotgun, but I always wanted to try out a real bow and arrow. Michael did that smile and nod thing he does that just makes things happen and I knew I'd be getting my Katniss on before the trip was over.

After dinner it was my turn to surprise Michael. When we got back to the room I told him to make himself comfortable on the couch in the den of our suite. We had eight full nights to spend together uninterrupted, and I was going to make up for all the nights we'd lost to business trips and games going into overtime. I'd overpacked for sure, extra boots and sweaters, long sleeves for the weather that was accurately predicted. But what Michael didn't know was that one of my bags was filled entirely with lingerie and fun accessories, like lube and our favorite butt plug. I even brought some wrist and ankles cuffs just in case we were feeling particularly adventurous.

I took my time changing, laying out every piece of my barely there outfit on the bed before I put them on. I touched up my lip gloss then finished the look off by putting my hair up in a ponytail. Fluffed out my bangs to the side. I grabbed some lube, the Michael dildo that was definitely going to require a nickname, and another toy that was more for setting the mood than anything else.

I peeked out the bedroom door at the back of Michael's head. He was looking down at his phone. Apparently I'd taken long enough that someone had enough time to come up and get the fireplace going. I took a deep breath and shook off my nerves.

"Baby, close your eyes."

Michael slipped his phone in his jacket pocket, then dropped his chin to his chest. "They're closed."

I slowly walked out into the living area and came around the couch. He was wearing one of my favorite suits. A deep navy blue that fit him so well. He was gonna have to get it dry cleaned for sure after tonight.

I set the lube and the dildo down on the coffee table between the sofa and the fireplace, then shifted the plush basketball under my arm, and struck the perfect pose.

"Okay, you can open them."

He slowly raised his lids and then made a little choking noise when he saw what I was wearing. I smiled and shifted my weight on my hip a little more. I knew how my curves looked.

"You're not the only one who stashed a few things in their luggage."

"You know I went and got a full physical a few weeks ago because I knew you would pull some shit like this. Sometimes I really think you're trying to kill me." He looked me up and down, taking in everything I wasn't wearing.

The extra small jersey the Flames' front office had given me when Michael bought the team had given me some ideas. I couldn't fit that tiny piece of fabric over my head. But that didn't mean I couldn't have another jersey custom made. This was black, the Away colors, and just barely covered my tits, but the geniuses I found for the work make it so the word FLAMES was on perfect display in double-mounted red and white. I turned around so he could get the full effect.

MRS. BRADBURY and the number two are crammed onto the back, but legible and in perfect proportion. They provided enough fabric so I could tie it in a little sexy knot off to the side. I praised the lord of plus size fashion for finally giving me more than one retailer that sold thigh-high athletic socks big enough to cover my ample thighs without bunching or cutting off my circulation. I picked out a white pair with the three red stripes at the top. A pair of red underwear with a thick white waistband and the imitation boy seams brought it all together.

I looked at Michael, biting my bottom lip. "I was hoping I could try out for the team."

His eyes darkened and then he spread his arms out across the back of the couch. We dabbled in role play, but it usually only lasted three seconds and there had never been costumes involved. I couldn't wait to bust out the Little Red Riding Hood Gone Slutty get up I had tucked in my suitcase.

"You missed the draft already," Michael said. "And camp. I could arrange a last minute try-out for you but you'd have to show me something really special."

"I swear I'm good. I have a mean chest pass and everything."

"I think it's going to take a little more than a chest pass to land a spot on this squad. Put that down—" he nodding toward the stuffed basketball. "And come here."

I set it down and stepped between his legs. He moved to the edge of the sofa. My hands automatically went to the back of his head. His hair was still a little damp from his pre-dinner shower. I gently tugged the soft strands, then massaged the base of his scalp. He looked up at me.

"Do you like it?" I asked.

"I like all of it."

I moaned as he moved closer and started kissing over my stomach. He turned me slowly, kissing every inch of available skin until I was facing the fireplace. I looked over my shoulder and could see from the look in his eye that he was gone, so far gone. It was gonna be a long night. I held still as he hooked his fingers into both sides of my underwear and pulled them up, exposing more of my ass cheeks. A little yelp slipped out as his teeth gently nipped at my sensitive skin. He kept going, biting and nipping, licking and kissing at my ass, my thighs, my hips.

"Grab your ankles. Grab the table," he nearly growled. "I don't care, just bend over and keep your legs together. Just like that. Good." The blood was rushing to my head, the heat from the fire warming the back of my neck as my ponytail just brushed the carpet, but I could clearly feel my pulse beating in my clit. I was already wet. The kisses and love bites turned me on more than I could have imagined. Michael stroked me, rubbing his fingers all over my pussy through the fabric of my panties. Over and over in firm but gentle circles. He was upside down from my vantage point, but the look on his face was so focused, so sexy, I was starting to lose patience.

"Baby?" I whined.

"Mhmmm?" He didn't look at me, just moved my underwear out of the way and slid a long finger into my cunt.

"I want you."

"You'll get me. All of me. Don't worry."

He toyed with me a while longer, finger fucking me until I couldn't stand it. Finally, when I felt like I was about to come, he took mercy on me and turned me around. He reached between my legs and readjusted my underwear again from the front. Still on, adding their splash of color for that extra bit of excitement, but out of the way for easy access. Then he reached for the dildo and the lube.

"Go get on the bed."

I knew what he was thinking. He was going to be too rough for the floor or the delicate sofa. Once I was in the other room, I sat down on the edge of the bed. I wanted him in every way. In my mouth, in my pussy, in my ass, and from the look on his face I knew I was going to get what I wanted, the way we both wanted it.

"Leave your suit on," I told him, squeezing my thighs together.

"Anything my wife wants." A little smile lifted his mustache. He tossed the lube beside me on the bed then took me by the chin with his free hand. "Open up."

My lips parted and he gently slid the dildo into my mouth. I knew it was fake, but sucking on it was almost as hot as sucking Michael's dick. He watched me for a few minutes as I used my lips and my tongue against his light pushes and pulls. He let out a deep breath through his nose and I knew he was reaching his limit. I lifted my hand and drew it over his erection, pressing against the crease in his dress pants.

Bobbing my head harder on the plastic cock, I gave his dick a light squeeze.

"Let's do a little switch," he said quietly. "I want this in your pussy."

"I want you in my mouth."

"I think that'll work best." That smile again. Devastating. He handed me the dildo and I wiggled all the way to the edge of the bed and opened my legs. I was so tight and swollen, hot and wet, pushing the toy between my inner lips felt so good. Michael gave me a few seconds to adjust to its size and its unyielding girth. He unzipped his pants and pulled out his cock. I didn't waste a second taking him in my mouth. I sucked his dick for a long time, savoring the taste of his leaking precum while I fucked myself with my new favorite toy. He closed his eyes, gripping the back of my head, no doubt loving the way my mouth felt on his body.

I could tell he was getting close when he stepped back and reached for the lube. "Get me ready."

"Butt stuff?" I teased. Michael didn't answer. He was too busy looking down at my hands spreading the lube around. When he was nice and slick he nodded for me to move up the bed, just enough to give him the room he needed to work. I let him take control of the dildo, lifting my hips to help him along. My eyes closed again when I felt his lube-slicked fingers moving around my ass and then he was pushing his way inside. It was a tight fit, especially with the dildo filling my pussy up so good, but like always, my body welcomed his any way I could get him.

Michael did all the work, fucking me deep and hard as I just laid back and played with my nipples. He started slow and gentle, measuring his thrusts, and the push and shove of the fake cock so he didn't hurt me, but soon I was begging. I wanted more, needed more. Faster and harder. At one point I opened my eyes and it was all too much. The dim lights of our honeymoon suite illuminating the lightly tanned skin of my gorgeous husband, still fully dressed in his perfectly tailored suit, and the sight of the wet spot that had spread all over the crotch of his pants. I took ahold of the dildo from him, calling out his name as I fucked myself rougher than I think he ever would.

I came, my eyes squeezing shut so hard I think I momentarily blacked out. It took a few seconds before I knew I was squirting, ejaculating on Michael's pants and cock and all over my own thighs. He froze for a moment, taking in the sight of what he had just done to me, and then he went back to work, pumping in and out until he groaned out his own orgasm, filling my ass with his cum. He called out my name, he told me how much he loved me. When we could both breathe again, there was a brief intermission. Michael cleaned up and got undressed and fished up something for us to drink. There was cuddling. Some kissing. He asked where I got the socks. We decided to name the dildo Mikey.

Chapter Three

The ten glorious days of our honeymoon went by way too fast. I wanted to cry as we drove away from our magical castle and our new best friend Gregory who absolutely hated me because I slipped and called him Greggy to his face. We did our fair share of hiding in our room, sleeping and screwing to our heart's content, but Michael actually had a lot of plans worked out for us. We joined a group at the archery range. Michael and I both actually had damn good aim once we got a hang of things, but my shoulders and arms were sore as shit the next day. There was talk of venturing out in search of a nightclub one night, but I was too tired for another adventure that required pants so Michael threw me a one man dance party. Watching him dance sort of on beat in his boxers was better than any bottle service or VIP section. I got to wear almost all of the sexy outfits I'd packed. Michael was partial to this lacy blue number and this slutty Snow White get up I'd found.

In the end though, with the slutty Little Red Riding Hood costume gone untouched, I was happy to head home. We had three weeks left in LA before we relocated to Miami for the NBA season. We tried to do the whole flying back and forth thing last season and made it about halfway through before I gave in and packed up the puppies so I could be with

Michael. Working remotely with Daniella and our team worked just fine, and she came to Miami whenever she felt like it so we could hang out. But Michael and I both still had a lot to do before we relocated back to Florida for the winter.

I knew the old adage that sometimes you need a vacation. I needed time to recover from our wedding and all the traveling, but I didn't realize how wiped I was until I went back into the office. The commute alone from Malibu to Santa Monica had me wanting to climb back into bed. And maybe it was all the changes and the travel and associated people germs, but I felt a little nauseated. I had to tell Patch to chill twice before I let him out of the car. I did not have the energy to keep up with him, but still I was excited to see the girls.

I slowly opened the door, trying to make a surprise dramatic entrance but Patch wouldn't be kept from his adoring public or his forgotten toys. He nearly ripped my arm off trying to get inside.

"Jesus. Will you wait?" I had to drop his leash to keep my fingers.

Welcomes from around the room. Lili damn near jumped out of her chair so she could collect Patch in her arms. Daniella met me in the middle of the room and we hugged like fools. Our shipping/office manager Jade just nodded at me. She was a woman of few words.

"I'm so glad you're back!" Daniella squealed.

"I am too. I missed you!"

Brittany our assistant was next in line, waiting for her own hug. I pulled her in tight. "Hey girl!"

"We all missed you," she added cheerfully. I didn't even make it to my desk to put down my things. The three of us collapsed on the couch. Patch came over, butt swinging wildly so he could slobber on his other favorite humans.

"I see someone's happy to be off house arrest and back in the office," Daniella laughed.

"Oh my god, you should have seen him and Penny when we got home. They both lost their shit."

"Of course they did," Daniella cooed, rubbing Patch's face. "They missed their mommy and daddy. I'm sure Holger lost his shit too. I don't know what he did without you."

"Enjoyed ten days of peace and quiet, and rethought ever going to work for Michael in the first place," I joked. "He was cranky as fuck, actually. I think he really missed us too. You know his game is sarcasm and—"

"He laid it on thick?"

"So, so thick. But whatever, we brought him presents and we brought you guys presents!" I reached down, opened the giant tote I had with me and pulled out the individually wrapped goods. A necklace for Lili and Brittany each and a stag brooch for Daniella, this cool keychain for Jade. I had no clue what she actually liked.

"There's more," I said as they tore open their gifts. "I got cheese, chocolates, like five boxes of whisky flights 'cause we're all a little productive when we're a bit tipsy."

Lili grabbed one of the boxes of chocolate. "I'm just gonna open this."

"So tell us," Daniella said. "How does it feel to be a married woman?"

"Good," I said in my most girly of voices. "I don't know, the wedding took up so much...energy. It felt like it would never come and maybe I was a little worried that it was such a distraction, like the circus of it all—"

"Oh, Infinity released their exclusives of your wedding." Lili pulled out her phone and started typing. "Here you go."

"Oooh." It was weird to see myself on a magazine's website. Shannon had sent over links to all the images she took that day, but there were nearly a thousand. I hadn't had time to go through them all. The pictures she picked for the spread were amazing.

"They're delivering the hard copies to your house," Brittany added.

"Add on to the mountain of shit I have to go through, no doubt. Anyway yeah, the wedding was one thing, but married life? It's been pretty good." Up close, I knew Daniella could tell I was blushing.

"Of course it is," she groaned. "I hatelove you two so much."

"How have things been here? What did I miss?"

"Business is still running. Orders are on schedule, though you've got a ton to approve."

"You do," Brittany added with a smile. "I made a list."

"Great. Can't wait. This is gonna be amazing. What else?"

"Duke and I broke up for good."

"What? What happened?" Daniella and her on-again off-again, I didn't even know what they were, had been at this as long as Michael and I had been together. But while we were racing forward, the two of them couldn't even seem to find a parking space outside the track.

"He cheated," Lili said.

"He did not," Daniella said, swatting at her little sister. "After you guys left the reception, some friend of a friend of a guest on Michael's side tried to kiss him."

"Did he kiss her back?"

"No, no and she was very drunk."

"So you just dumped him?"

"I...thought long and hard about what our relationship will be like long term and I am adult enough to know that I do not have the stomach to date an actual famous person. It really is too much."

"Okay," I said with a sigh. "But I vote no on this whole proposition." I loved them both and if they could just both stop being so ridiculous...

"That's what I said." Lili was just as confused as I was.

"I'm here if you want to talk about it."

"I'm locking down all Duke related emotions nice and tight, but don't worry," Daniella said. "I'll come to you when I have my inevitable breakdown."

I couldn't help but laugh. "Please do. What's new with you?" I said to Brittany. She started bouncing in her seat as soon as she had my full attention. "Oh god. What is it?"

"If we can just move to your desk. I can show you on your calendar."

"Fuck. Yeah let me actually work. I think a month off is more than enough. Eat all the food, drink all the whisky. When we get a few spare minutes, we'll call Michael on speaker and I'll have him do his new Scottish accent for you. It's terrible."

I threw my hands up, ending our a.m. party, then Brittany gave me the rundown on everything she needed approval for and meetings and calls she needed approval to set up. And designs, designs, designs that needed to be approved. The holidays were right around the corner. I was glad I enjoyed the fuck out of my honeymoon. I wasn't getting another break until after St. Patrick's day.

It took me almost three hours to get through my first round of catch up. No idea if it was the jetlag or what but when Brittany popped up at my desk again, I felt like my head was on backwards.

"Daniella says you're buying us lunch," she joked. Sort of. "What can I get you?" She handed me a menu to the sandwich shop around the corner. I scanned the sheet. Nothing looked good.

"The Coastal and the chicken soup 'cause I'm feeling extra fancy."

"Sounds good. Are you okay?" she asked.

It wasn't until someone said something that I realized I wasn't but I was still three-hundred emails away from the bottom of my inbox. Taking a break hadn't occurred to me. I stretched my neck and looked at my phone. There was a text from Michael.

"I do feel a little out of it, but I'll be fine." Blinking extra hard, I actually read his text as Brittany headed back to her desk.

> *Haven't seen you in six hours.*
> *We're still married right?*

The text was so cute, and for some reason, made me tear up. I got weepy when I was overtired.

> *Nope.* I texted back. *Found a new man. Sorry.*
> *I miss you. Come pick me up. I don't want to be a small business owner anymore.*

He texted me back right away.

> *I'll send a car.*

I knew he was joking, but suddenly I wished he wasn't. I didn't know what the fuck was wrong with me, but all I wanted was to be with him, in his arms. His next text didn't help at all. A picture of his left hand popped up. I looked at his shiny platinum band, then down at my own, ringed with diamonds.

> *I got distracted during a meeting just now. Keep checking out my new hardware.*

"Kay. Hey. Kayla." I looked up to see Daniella staring at me.

"Yeah?" I whipped my head up, realizing a second too late that I was wiping my eyes.

"You alright?" Lili was looking at me too and Brittany had turned back around.

"Yeah. I'm fine." I let out a slightly unhinged laugh. "I actually think I'm legit PMSing and I'm exhausted. Ignore me please." I grabbed the tissues that Jade was kind enough to order because, even though Daniella and I had worked out the kinks with payroll and all manner of shipping options, we forgot to get basics like Kleenex until she came on board. "Plus I'm just hangry. I barely ate any breakfast."

The girls all smiled at me and returned to their work. I hid behind my monitor. It took me another five minutes to get my shit together.

There are long days and then there is your first day back to work after your honeymoon. Lunch did not help at all. I was dragging ass through the rest of the afternoon, counting down the minutes till I could call it quits for all of us and still give off some sort of impression that I was actually taking my job seriously. Which I was, but oh my god, I wanted to go home. A nap was so called for and I really, really wanted to see Michael. But when Patch and I walked through the door, Holger was waiting for us like he was ready to stage an intervention.

"What's that look?" I asked him when I walked into the kitchen.

"You told me to remind you. Thank-you notes." He pointed toward the mountain of wedding gifts waiting on and around the living room table.

"Oh come on maannn," I groaned.

"Don't come on man, me—" fucking hilarious with his German accent. "The thank you cards you special ordered already arrived and you gave me specific instructions."

"Well I have to wait for Michael to come home before I can crack into these anyway." And of course I heard the garage open and close, and Penny's tags as she sprinted to be reunited with her buddy. Michael walked around their butt sniffing and he smiled when he realized Holger and I were having another one of our showdowns.

"Don't even bother, man. Whatever it is you want, you're not gonna get if it means me going against her," he laughed.

"We have to open gifts and get started on the thank you cards, but I don't want to. I just want you to hold me." I walked into his arms and buried myself under his chin. I may have glared at Holger.

"I wasn't hired to teach either of you ettique. Your dinner is ready."

Michael laughed even harder and pulled me closer. I knew he wanted a kiss, but I wanted to cling to him a few seconds more. "Hey what's going on?"

"I think I'm going crazy. I think you broke me."

"Come sit." He took my hand and pulled me over to the island stools while Holger pulled our dinner out of the oven. My mouth instantly started watering as I sat and turned to face my husband. He reached up, smoothed back my hair, kissed me on my temple and then my lips. He kissed me again, longer this time. "What's going on? How was work?"

"Work was fine. It was nice to see the girls and we got an order from this woman who runs a small gay bookstore in Louisiana. She wants to carry the Queer Qards." We'd already done one big deal with a larger distributor, but the smaller orders made my day.

"That sounds great. What's got you wanting to fight Holger?"

"Nothing. 'Cause he knows I'd mop the floor with him," I teased. Holger rolled his eyes at me. "I just felt weird today. Like tired, but almost lonely? I couldn't put my finger on it. I don't feel like myself. I googled 'Is it normal to miss your spouse after your honeymoon?'."

Michael huffed a little laugh. "Any good results?"

"Fifteen pages on what to do when the honeymoon period of your relationship is over and an article about a woman whose husband just dipped on her for five days during their honeymoon."

"Sounds like a classy guy. If it helps any, I missed you too. Ruben kept making fun of me because I was either looking at my ring or our engagement picture on my desk."

"I started crying after you texted me that picture."

"Ah, baby." Another kiss helped a little. I went in for another just for good measure.

"I'm that weird woman, aren't I? Twelve hours apart and wandering around Third Street Promenade asking people if they've seen my Michael."

"You know what I think?"

"What's that?"

"That a lot of people are cynical about love and so maybe we're conditioned to think we're being foolish when we care for someone else so much. But I also think that I waited a really long time to find the perfect woman for me, so if I'm so amazed that she wants to spend her life with me that it makes me pause to stare at this little symbol of that love every three and a half minutes or so, those cynical people can kiss my ass."

"So how do I go on being a functioning member of society when I seriously want to spend every minute of my day with you?"

"Well let's see, we can increase our texting exponentially."

Holger set down two helpings of beef Wellington with impressive looking greens in front of us. My stomach growled as we thanked him.

"There's that. We could text more," I said, digging into my dinner. I moaned and gave Holger the thumbs up. He was such a punk sometimes but he cooked his ass off. Michael took a few bites of his own before he went on.

"I can sell the team and retire, and you can work on K&D from home."

"Nooo don't do that. It's cool that you own a basketball team and now that we're married, I kinda own it too. Don't sell my team."

"Then I think we're just gonna have to spend all of our free time together joined at the hip."

"I know what we can do." I put down my fork and turned my whole body toward him. "Oh this'll be good."

"I'm listening."

"Well we do a lot of stuff together, but most of the time it's work related, for you at least. I think our honeymoon was so great because this last year was so busy we couldn't just stop and have it just be us."

"That is true."

"How about we extend our honeymoon. Keep doing fun romantic stuff together for a whole year and then for our anniversary, we'll go on a super date?"

"A super date you say."

"Shut up. Seriously. Let's make a point to do something special together once a week. Just us. We'll call 'em honey dates."

"I think we can do that."

"Good. I'll make a list of fun coupley stuff for us to do after dinner."

Holger spun around at the sink. I thought he might kill us both.

"After we open some gifts and send some thank you notes," I added. That seemed to get him to chill the fuck out. For the moment.

We devised a plan, mostly because I wasn't gonna let Holger ruin all my fun. I'd unwrap and Holger would keep a spreadsheet of who the gifts were from and Michael would make the list of HoneyDates we wanted to go on. Fifty-two, give or take, rocking romancey dates just for me and my man.

"What have we got so far?" I asked Michael as Holger handed me a box that weighed a freaking ton.

"From Adam Reynolds."

"God, what is in here? A body?"

I set the box down gently, careful not to break the coffee table. Adam Reynolds was another master of tech. Where Michael had the app game covered, Adam was in the business of hardware. He'd added Cyclone's Vortex smart watches to our goodie bags in the gifting suite. That was more than enough, plus his son, Blake and Blake's fiancée, my buddy Tina had already given us a beautiful painting. I couldn't imagine what else Adam could want to give to us. I opened the card. I read it once and then read it again out loud for Michael.

You bitched and moaned when I threatened to toss you off the store if you didn't convert your shit to 64-bit architecture, but I was fucking right. I'm always right.

Michael just shook his head and laughed.

"I assume this is just for you?"

"He's such an ass. Go ahead and open it."

I pulled back the paper and unwrapped a sixty-four piece tool kit. "Oh I'm keeping this. We don't have tools at the Miami house."

"What are you going do with those?" Michael asked, his eyebrow almost hitting his hairline.

"Build things. That's what. You can write his thank-you note. Let's switch." I took Michael's laptop and handed him my lap board and stationary.

He had a shared doc up with HONEYDATES FUCK YEAH in bold at the top.

I read down all the things we'd discussed: bowling, drive in, wine tasting, cooking classes, more picnics 'cause the one we shared in Scotland was a-maze-balls, the opera, and karaoke downtown. There were two items with question marks. Horseback riding—I told him to put a pin in that. The other was tattoos, which we hadn't discussed.

"Babe? You wanna get tattoos together?"

He stopped the mad scribbling he doing and looked up. He shrugged. "I was planning to get a little something to commemorate our wedded bliss. Thought maybe you'd be game."

Michael had one massive tattoo that spanned his right side, front and back. I was ink free.

"Yeah, I think we could do that. What were you thinking of getting?"

"Well, I wanted it to be a surprise."

"For your wife?"

"For my wife."

"Yeah, okay we can do that. Did you schedule something already?"

"I did. For this weekend."

"Oh?"

"Don't worry, it won't interfere with our date. I'll call Sophea and see if she can squeeze you in too. You're not gonna get a whole back piece are you?"

"Ah no."

"She'll be cool. I'll email her tonight."

"Does it count as a date if you already had it on the books?" I said, crawling forward to kiss him. It had been an hour since our mouths had touched. I thought I might die.

"After, I'll take you to dinner and a movie. How about that?"

"I think it's a date."

Chapter Four

By Friday I'd caught up on most of my work, and Michael and I had made a dent in the gift pile. I was feeling pretty accomplished until Holger reminded us that Vera was hanging on to another four dozen or so gifts at the Miami house. Those people were just going to have to wait. Friday night, Michael had dinner plans with his business partner Steven and someone who wanted them to invest in something or other. But Saturday was our first HoneyDate. His tattoo artist Sophea only had Michael on the books for that day. I had no idea what massive piece he was getting this time, but she said she would absolutely ink me up. Daniella helped me brainstorm ideas. We settled on a candy heart with Michael's name in the middle, stippling style.

"I know you're not supposed to tattoo someone's name on you," she said, laughing even though she was dead serious. "But if he does something really stupid they are doing amazing things with cover-ups these days." She was right, thank you Tattoo Nightmares for showing us the way, but I had a feeling I would never regret it.

I let Holger bully me into sending out ten more thank-you notes and then I had to call it quits. I still hadn't recovered from our trip. Actually I was starting to feel even more worn out. I wanted to wait up for Michael to get home from dinner but there was just no way. I climbed into bed with the dogs around nine and I was out.

At 2:33 am I jumped out of bed, ran to the bathroom and threw up. I couldn't remember the last time I'd been physically ill, maybe high school when I had food poisoning, but this was something else. I was dead asleep and the next thing I knew, I was sprinting for the bathroom. I think I knew, in the back of my head, but puking in the middle of a REM cycle when I was bone tired had my body on autopilot. I needed more rest. My body needed to be horizontal again. I came back to bed and felt my way around in the ambient light from the backyard. Michael asked me if I was okay. I think I mumbled something like "Yeah, I'm fine." I wiggled back under his arm and even though my whole body felt like I'd just done the electric slide through a car wash, I fell back to sleep.

We didn't have to be at Sophea's shop until noon, so Michael let me sleep in. He was already up and out of the bedroom when I got up. I took a long time getting ready. I felt a little better, but still really strange. I was afraid I was going to be sick again. When I came into the living room, I found that the rest of the gifts were unwrapped and Holger and Michael were organizing them. An impressive display, but all I could focus on was the smell of whatever Holger had made for breakfast and fresh coffee. My throat clenched.

Michael glanced at me, then went back to whatever he was tinkering with. "Hey babe, we knocked all the rest out. I already wrote notes for the random business people who you don't actually know. You just have to sign those and then we put the ones we knew you'd want to personalize over here."

It was so thoughtful and later when I could think straight I would really appreciate it, but instead of thanking them both, I walked straight over to Michael and put my hand on his side. He turned on reflex and pulled me closer to his side. He kissed my face.

"Good morning. What's up?" he said and then his smile immediately dropped. I knew exactly what my face looked like. "Holg, man, give us a second."

Holger nodded then did his usual disappearing act when Michael and I needed to talk privately. When I couldn't hear his footsteps in the hallway anymore I looked up at Michael.

"I think I'm pregnant."

"Oh. Okay," he said cautiously. I appreciated that he was leaving all his emotions at the door because I was freaking out. "Is that what happened last night?"

"Yeah, I threw up, but it wasn't normal. And I've been really tired. I've been really tired and rundown since before the wedding. I thought it was just all the planning and running around and small talk with relatives, but now I don't."

"Okay, well I can cancel with Sophea. We'll stay home and you can rest, and I'll make some calls, get you in to see your doctor." I had a GP but I hadn't been in to see her in a minute. "Is your period late?"

I thought back to my most current pack of birth control. My period was due next week, but… "I think I actually skipped my last one and the one before that was kinda light. I just thought it was stress. Shit, I am so sorry." I was already kinda warm and out of it, but then I felt a sudden rush of heat and dread flood over me. I was such an idiot.

"Hey, hey. It's okay. Let's find out for sure, okay? Could just be some weird Scottish flu. Maybe no need to panic."

"Okay."

"And even if you are pregnant, still no need to panic. Okay?"

"Yeah. Okay. Yeah. You're right."

"Do you want to go get back in bed? Holger made waffles and bacon, but we can get you something lighter?"

I realized then that even though I was feeling kinda meh, I didn't feel like I needed my German housekeeper to tuck me in with my blankie. My body was vibrating and my brain was taking a weird trip into the past, analyzing all the moments that qualified me for an episode of I Didn't Know I Was Pregnant, but I was okay. I could be up and about. I could leave

the house. And Michael did have a point, it was best
to know for sure before I started freaking out.

"No, I'm fine. I think I'll just have some cereal
and then we can go."

"You sure?"

"Yes. I'm positive. HoneyDate is still on.
Besides, Sophea cleared her whole day for us. It
would be pretty shitty to cancel last minute. If I feel
pukey, I'll let you know."

"Okay, one thing though. If you are pregnant—
"

"I shouldn't get a tattoo."

"You shouldn't get a tattoo."

"Let me eat and then we'll stop at CVS on the
way." I was gonna pee on a stick.

Sophea earned herself some major sisterhood points.
As soon as we got to the tattoo parlor I explained to
her what happened. She totally understood and told
me not to worry, then pointed me toward the
bathroom. She'd tattoo me whenever I was ready.
Apparently I was the fifth person to take a pregnancy
test in that shop, that she knew of.

The first test didn't even give me time to think.
I set the timer on my phone, but the little display
flashed PREGNANT after like ten seconds. I used
the other test and got the same result just as fast.

Yeah, false positives and all that shit, but I highly doubted it. I buried the tests under a few paper towels in the trash, then headed back out to the lobby. Music was blasting from the back of the shop where I imagined Sophea was getting set up.

Michael was waiting on the bench, head hanging down, deep in thought. I almost didn't want to tell him, like I might ruin his day if it was true. Or ruin his life. He looked up as I came closer. His expression was completely unreadable.

"Well?"

"Yup." I clapped my hands together then rubbed my thighs. "Looks like no tattoo for me."

He held his hand out for me and then pulled me down on the bench beside him. "You okay?"

"Honestly I don't know. I think you're gonna have to do the processing for us both."

"Well let's look at this in parts. First part, we go see the doctor on Monday."

"And the next part?"

"That's up to you."

It took me a second to get what he was getting at. I sighed and slumped against him. "No, this is definitely happening."

"If you're not ready now or ever, I understand." We'd talked about kids. Planned kids. For exactly three years from now. But now was happening. There was no matter of wanting or planning anymore. It was game time.

"I'm ready," I said, which I was. "Just really surprised." Which I really fucking was.

"Can I tell you something?"

"Of course." I slid my hand down his thigh and wiggled his knee. "Tell me."

"I've been processing a little for myself since this morning."

"And?"

"I'm excited."

"You are?"

He just nodded. Sometimes it was really easy for me to forget that Michael had done a lot of living before he met me. We came together at the perfect moment in both our lives, but I wasn't dealing with some stupid teen boy who thought the pull out method was foolproof. This was Michael, my husband, and my husband always meant what he said. I wasn't sure I could breathe and I was not looking forward to puking again. And the however many times after that, but I did want this baby and I wanted it with him. Knowing that he was excited? That was exactly what I needed to hear.

Sophea found us tangled up in an emotional mess. Somehow I'd ended up on Michael's lap, weeping tears of happiness and utter terror into his hair.

"So we going for one or two today?" she asked with a sheepish smile.

"One," I said, making a half-ass attempt at wiping my face. I forced myself to dismount so Michael and Sophea could get to work. He took my hand and we followed her to a large, but closed-off area in the back. There was techno-y hip hop playing. I took a seat in an armchair Sophea had pulled in for me and listened while they made small talk as Michael took off his shirt and got the left side of his chest shaved. Apparently the two of them had been working on the design for months, a massive piece done in stippling style of a heart, an array of flowers and my name appearing in the negative space. Below the second A, she'd added a lip print. I stood over Michael's bare chest after Sophea invited me to come take a look. Something caught my eye.

"Are those my lips?" I asked him. "They look bigger than your standard."

"They are," he said.

"Um how did you manage that? Did Holger dust the glasses for a viable print?"

"I'm sure he would have pulled something we could've worked with, but no. Daniella did me a solid."

I stared at him for a long moment as this doofy smile fought against the weight of that stupid, sexy mustache. And then I remembered. The smile won when I gasped. Like four months before, Daniella had brought in a ton of lipstick samples Duke had sent her to see which she liked best 'cause some designer offered to hook up every woman in his life with free shit. Anyway, we wasted a good hour in the office giggling and kissing different pieces of paper because we're twelve and had no business running our own company and being in charge of things. I figured all the papers had ended up in the trash.

"You and Daniella stop conspiring to be cute behind my back."

"We'll try, but no promises."

Sophea let us know she was ready and I figured maybe she didn't need me standing over her the whole time she worked. Michael had been forward thinking enough to remind me to bring my tablet, but once I saw the design, even though it took hours, it was hard to look away. I did look away for a moment though to give Daniella a piece of my mind.

You stole my lip print? Do you steal used condoms too? I texted her. She answered right away.

Is he getting the tattoo???? There were sixteen smiley faces in a row and then a *And that is disgusting.* with a laughing smiley face.

He is. You traitor. Stop being such a good friend. By the way I'm pregnant.

And then I turned off my phone, just to give her a taste of what suspense is really like. I shoved my phone in my bag and watched Sophea work her magic.

Aside from our couple tattoo sesh turning into a solo inking, HoneyDate 1 of 52 went off with only a few hiccups. I only had to sprint to the bathroom twice, but at least I made it to the bathroom. The shop manager ran out and got me some mint tea and biscotti to nibble on and that actually seemed to help. But even though I felt like garbage, I couldn't have asked for a better day. Watching Michael get tattooed, like a big ass fucking tattoo of my name—and my lips—was so damn romantic. The fact that he was looking at me nearly the whole time, like he loved me a whole hell of a lot wasn't helping things. We were going to have a baby. Together. I was terrified but I couldn't be happier. I only cried three times before Sophea declared she was done. Dinner and a movie turned into me trying to keep down broth as we watched an advance copy of the upcoming DC movie in the screening room with the puppies snoozing beside us.

Holger, that ass, intuited that something was up and filled the fridge with stuff the Internet told him would be good to combat morning sickness.

We spent the rest of the weekend in. Responded to Daniella's eighty texts and ten calls.

Michael and I talked a lot. I cried a lot, mostly happy tears, but I seriously could not stop. I was happy. Michael was happy. He wouldn't stop touching my stomach, which made me happier 'cause it was so stinking cute. Daniella was happy. Holger was suddenly over attentive and frazzled and that made me even happier. I knew our families would be happy as soon as we told them. I told Michael we would as soon as I saw my doctor. And I wasn't going into the office again until we did. I didn't want to face the girls again until I had proof. And pictures.

There is something so, so awful about doctors' offices. It didn't matter what you were there for, it always feels like it's going to be bad news. Dr. Zelner was too perky for my liking. Mostly because I felt like shit wrapped in garbage and Michael has spent nearly the whole ride to the hospital making horrible jokes in his horrible Scottish accent because he knew I secretly loved it, but I could pretend he was annoying me so I'd have another reason to be so fucking cranky.

I did my best not to fidget too much as Dr. Zelner explained that I was indeed pregnant and it was time to have a look. I stared at the ceiling as the nurse, who was very sweet and could tell I wanted to get the fuck out of there, prepped my belly for the show and tell. Then Michael muttered a frightening "Oh shit."

"What!? Don't do that. What?" I said as I looked at the monitor. And then I saw what he saw, but I wasn't ready to believe it. There was no fucking way.

"It looks like..." The nurse prodded some more. "Yeah, it looks like twins. There is baby number one and baby number two." She pointed to the screen and then smiled at me. At least I think she did. I had entered an alternate dimension where sights and sounds and maybe even colors didn't exist. The color had definitely drained out of Michael's face. He managed to stay upright. It was a good thing I was already lying down.

The nurse did some stuff, printed something, then left us with her congratulations and the cheerful Doctor.

"Any twins in the family?" he asked gleefully. I wanted to kill him suddenly and Michael too. And maybe my mom and my grandmother.

"Yeah," I squeaked out. I cleared the rage out of my throat and tried to answer again. "Yes. My mom is a twin and my little sisters are twins. They are identical too." A complete accident. But this? Maybe a coincidence, but I doubted it. This ran in the family.

"Well it looks like you're about ten weeks along."

"Ten?"

"What?!"

Michael and I said at the same time. I looked at him and then let my head flop back on that horrible hospital table paper.

"Game seven," I muttered. Michael just nodded. He knew. The Flames had already been knocked out of the tournament but we'd flown to Sacramento for the final, gotten super fucked up and had the wildest drunken sex in our hotel room.

"You said the morning sickness just started?"

"Yeah on Friday night."

"I'd expect a little sooner if it was coming at all, but every pregnancy is different. Everything looks fine. I'm going to want to see you pretty frequently. Twins are nothing to worry about, but since your body is working double time we'll want to keep an eye on things."

"Oh, um," Michael sort of stammered and then he cleared his throat. "We might need a referral."

"Oh god, yeah. We *winter* in Miami," I said, rolling my eyes.

"I'm not surprised. I follow the league. I'm a fan." My eyes narrowed as he looked between Michael and I, pearly whites gleaming. Our Dr. Zelner was actually fanboying over Michael. I didn't even bother to fix my face when he looked back at me. "We'll get you a great referral. You'll probably deliver there before the season's over."

Still fanboying. He said some other stuff about my weight and the possibility of babies forcing me to lose a few pounds as I went along, but I had already checked out. I knew I was the patient, but I was glad Michael was there to be properly polite as we made our way out with first snapshots and a DVD of our babies.

"I didn't know your mom was a twin," Michael said as we pulled out of the parking lot.

"She is. Fraternal. You met my uncle Calvin at the wedding."

"Oh."

"And my grandma and her sister. And my great grandma. Oh my god."

"Baby, it's okay."

"You can lie to yourself right now. Not me, okay? I was almost ten when my mom was pregnant with Kaleigh and Kiara. I remember everything. It was not pleasant."

"It's gonna b—" he stopped himself when I glared at him like I was completely prepared to deal with the repercussions of pushing him out of the car into oncoming traffic.

I pulled the pictures out and took a picture of the clearest one. There were definitely two babies.

I typed *I am so pissed at you and grandma right now.* And then remembered my mom might actually come through the phone if I spoke to her that way. I tried again.

I know you miss Kaleigh and Kiara—sophomore year of college had just started for them—*But it's grandma time.*

I sent *that* text to my mom along with the picture. Even though she was at work at the bank, she called me right back.

"You're pregnant?!" She practically screamed when I said hello.

"Yeah," I said. And then I grabbed the bag Michael had been smart enough to bring along with us, and threw up.

Chapter Five

Telling my mom I was pregnant was like activating a sleeper agent. I thought she was excited to plan her first wedding, but grandkids? She was fucking ret tuh go. I convinced her that we could save this conversation for later that night, when I wasn't retching in the car and when she wasn't on the clock. But the second she got home from work, she blew up my phone. She had fifty thousands questions, all of which I had to answer because I knew she'd go into full nagging mode and start drilling Michael for details or worse, she'd fly out. I confirmed that yes, indeed we were having twins, that I was ten weeks along and yes, I'd been barfing more than I'd appreciate. She was ready though, tips and home remedies out the ass.

I was listening, taking mental notes, but there was something in my mom's tone that I couldn't ignore. The initial excitement was gone, replaced by genuine curiosity and concern. She was always in mom mode, but sometime after Michael and I announced our engagement she really started treating me like my own person, like she'd finally acknowledged my receipt of my grown woman pants.

She'd be on one of her slightly instructive overprotective tears and then something would shift and she'd ask me about Michael's mom or what plans we had for Easter like she was asking me woman to woman. She'd stopped worrying about the age gap between me and Michael, accepted that he had a different kind of common sense because his money hadn't been given to him at birth. He'd worked for it. She was always worried that one of his older, rich white associates would say something sideways to me, but at some point she'd given in to actually trusting us as a unit, and now as a married couple.

For me, there was knowing I was pregnant and then there's understanding that I was really going to be a parent. In that moment, my own mother was talking to me mom to mom and I felt it. Another shift.

"The doctor said everything is fine, but he wants me to keep my weight up."

"Oh yeah. I had the same problem. All I could keep down was mashed potatoes from KFC and I started wasting away. But it was fine. Just get plenty of rest. Don't do too much running around."

"I just wasn't expecting this, I guess," I told her. "I'm still kind of in wedding mode."

"Yeah, but these things happen. You can still enjoy being a new bride and a new mom. Double the joy," she said. We talked some more. She had a few more tips about the joint pain and other fun, gross chronic stuff I had to look forward to, but she seemed satisfied with the current situation. She was ready to grandma.

I almost succeeded in getting her off the phone, but then my dad came home and had his own round of questions. Then he wanted to speak to Michael who had regained function of his facial features but was still an interesting shade of white.

My dad must have said some funny dude to dude thing 'cause Michael laughed and suddenly seemed like he'd been snapped out of the trance. They talked a few minutes more. Michael paced the whole time, alternating between rubbing the back of his head and lightly touching his healing tattoo through his shirt. Lots of "Yeahs," and there was an "I get it" and a "No, we haven't gotten to that point yet."

"You still think it's gonna be fine?" I asked when they hung up. I knew I was being an asshole, but I couldn't help it. So many emotions. He glared at me a brief second then came to join me on the couch. I glared back at him when he gently started playing with my fingers.

"I know things are going to be fine. You have me. You have both our families and Daniella and Holger and Vera. Ruben and the girls. These babies already have a whole team behind them."

"Yeah, there's that."

"And even though we wanted to wait a little while, I think we'll be able to provide for them. I have a little money saved up and even though things might be a little tight, we can turn one of the eight rooms we have here and at the Miami house into a nursery. There might even be room in one of the backyards for a swing set. If we really pull the purse strings tight maybe we'll be able to afford to get them bikes one day."

"Shut up."

He leaned forward and kissed my cheeks. "That's what I mean when I say it's gonna be fine. I'm gonna make sure you have everything you need and then I'm going to spoil the shit out of them. Let me and the whole gang take care of you and you just worry about yourself and the precious cargo."

"You're not even just lowkey excited, are you? You're terrified, yet you are pumped."

"Yeah. Your dad said I have the easy job. I get to have all the fun. He said it's even better if we have girls. I'll always get to good cop."

"Yes. These are things I've considered. Let's get through the first trimester and then we can talk about how much our unborn children are going to hate me by default."

"Ohhh come here. I didn't mean it like that." I let him hug me and kiss all on me, but still. "How are you doing? Tell me," he said. He shifted so he could cuddle me properly without my whole back pressing against his fresh ink.

"I'm feeling like—lost. I feel lost. Like I'm having an out of body experience. Like definitely pregnant. Definitely feeling that, but also feeling like I should have known and kind of like an idiot because I was exhausted as shit our whole honeymoon and I chalked it up to jetlag. But also...maybe like I shouldn't be beating myself up about it?"

"You definitely shouldn't."

I turned and faced him. "Let's have sex tonight."

"We can do that if you're feeling up to it." I leaned into his palm as he brushed my hair away from my cheek.

"I can't decide if I'm mad at you and your stupid sperm or if I'm just anxious for the obvious reasons. But you're touching me right now and having a conference between my crotch and your dick and balls is all I can think of."

"I will be sure to rise to the occasion."

"I heard the libido thing is off the charts second and third trimester. Get ready."

"What are we preparing for?" Holger said as he walked into the kitchen. His arms were loaded down with packages.

"What are those?" I asked.

"More wedding gifts, I imagine."

"Fuck that life. I'll let you two get cracking on those." I stood and kissed Michael on the cheek. "I'll be in bed contemplating my whole existence."

"I have some work to finish up, but I'll be in in a bit. Go ahead."

"What are we preparing for?" Holger asked again.

"Twins, bro," I said with some jazz hands as I walked toward our bedroom. Michael's snort of laughter finally made me smile.

We didn't have sex that night. I was in a coma when Michael came to bed and whether he tried to wake me up or not, the sex was not happening. Even though I was feeling better, he insisted PJ drive me and Patch to the office in the morning. Doctor Fanboy assured me that there would be unpredictable morning sickness for the duration of this slow descent into madness. Catching a ride didn't seem like a bad idea.

I didn't even try to sneak into the office all cute like I was gonna get away with not talking about this for even one second. I just threw open the door for Patch and stormed in.

"I'm back, bitches. Who wants to see pictures of my insides?"

"Oh, thank God." Daniella jumped up from her desk. She rushed over and tugged me to the couch. "The suspense was killing me. Tell us everything."

Lili followed and took her usual seat on my right side. Brittany wasn't far behind. Jade seemed only moderately interested, and she stayed at her desk.

"So definitely pregnant," Daniella said.

"Oh yeah. *Supre* pregnant," I said as I pulled out my laptop and brought up the video Michael had been sweet enough to upload for me. He knew Daniella too well.

"I feel like every time you come into the office now, you have life-altering news," Lili said in her nearly monotone way.

"Well let's hope nothing else happens. I haven't even changed my name on my driver's license yet and I have to start thinking about mom things. Shudder. There." I pressed play on the little clip and then pointed to the screen. "Baybay One and Baybay A."

"Wait." Daniella said back, looking like she was about to slap me. "Two?"

"Yup."

"And you went a whole twenty-four hours without telling me?!"

"I'm still waiting for the other half of my brain to process the news."

"Kay! Oh my god." She threw her arms around me, then held me at arm's length. "Are you excited? Are you okay? Is Michael okay? Oh my god."

"We're both fine. Still in shock, but fine."

"Yay, yay, yay." She clapped her hands and bounced on the cushion beside me. "First a wedding, now baby stuff. I love this kind of shopping."

"Lemme see?" Jade slowly made her way over. I pressed played for her, pointing out the two separate sacks again.

"Trippy. Bodies are weird, dude. Congrats." Jade patted me on the back and went back to her desk.

"Can I name one?" Lili asked.

"Excuse me?" Daniella said. "If anyone gets naming rights—"

"Today's my last day!" Brittany blurted out.

"What?"

"Huh?"

"Your what?" I put down my laptop and turned to face Brittany who was standing a few feet behind the couch suddenly, like she'd been backing away from us.

"You're quitting?" I asked.

"Yeah. I, um—I'm so sorry. I just didn't know how to tell you."

"Um, what happened?"

"Yeah, why are you leaving?" Daniella asked. "Is it something we can at least talk about first?"

Brittany was really young, but she was smart and organized as hell. She was a perfect foil for Lili and Jade with the upbeat energy she brought to our workspace. I really liked her.

She started crying. "I'm going away with Chris. We met at your wedding and really hit it off."

"Which Chris?" Lili muttered the right question. Michael was friends with every A-list Chris in Hollywood and all but one made it to our wedding. I knew the one she was talking about, though. I'd seen them talking at the reception.

"He's going to Morocco to shoot a movie and he asked me to come with him."

"Uh, and what about when you get back? You won't need a job when you get back?" Daniella asked gently.

"We're gonna play it by ear. I know it sounds stupid, but look at you two. You married your rich Prince Charming. And Daniella, you know that Duke would whisk you away at the drop of a hat. Neither of you need this company."

"She's got you there," Lili said.

"Stop," Daniella grumbled at her sister. "There's a slight difference there though, Brit. Neither of us quit our jobs to run after Duke or Michael."

"But Kayla was unemployed when she met Michael, that's what you said." She looked at me, eyes pleading like I was gonna suddenly run to her defense.

My mouth popped open. And then I closed it and scrubbed my cheek. "I'm gonna get some air. Daniella, care to join me?"

"Sure."

I grabbed Patch's leash and we followed him out as he booked it to the door.

As soon as we were outside, I spun on Daniella. "Is she fucking serious?"

"I don't know. Sounds like it. What do we do?"

"What can we do? She already quit. You want to talk her out of going? 'Cause I kinda don't. But I mean, give us a little heads up."

"Yeah, not so professional. Yeah...shit. There's nothing we can do. We can have her write her own job listing before she leaves."

"I'll do it. I want her to make sure she gives us everything, and I mean every contact, email, vendor, everything before six o'clock."

"That's fair. You're kinda sexy when you get all bossy."

"I'll take that compliment and hold on to it for when I can't see my feet anymore."

"She really thinks this is gonna turn out like you and Michael. I guess it could happen. Chris is pretty nice."

"Yeah nice and like, allergic to monogamy. He came to our wedding with his fifth supermodel of the year."

"True. And he's not Michael."

I turned up my nose and flipped my hair over my shoulder. "That is true. I can't believe she said that though. I mean, I know Michael and Duke are amazing, but this?"

"I know, I know. I didn't like that either. And it's really not the same thing. Let's go back inside and try not to choke her."

"In a minute. Patch is doing the dance."

After my puppy had gotten his fill of the parking lot's shrubbery, we went back in. Daniella sat with Brittany and after she got her to stop apologizing, they started transferring everything she had stored on her laptop and her brain.

I texted Michael. *Chris stole our assistant. Brittany is running away with him to Morocco.*

He answered right away.

Which Chris?!!

I smiled and started texting him again, but then of course what's an hour in my life without a little action.

"Um, Kayla?" Lili said.

"What now?"

She messaged me the link. A gossip site. I knew this was gonna be good. I clicked it and sure enough. There was a picture of Michael and I leaving the hospital under the headline ***EXPECTING ALREADY??'*** Thank god Zia had taught me a great five-minute-paparazzi-face so I didn't look like pure shit. But what the fuck?

"Kay?" Lili must have sent the link to Daniella too.

"I'm fine."

And I was, or would be as soon as I made another high-speed trip to the bathroom.

Michael found me out in the cabana with the puppies. It was a perfectly cool night and the wifi signal was strong, and it was impossible to surf gossip sites and watch Netflix at the same time. We'd wrapped things up with Brittany and sent her on her way with our best wishes. After PJ drove me home, I'd showered just to wash away some of the tension I was holding in my neck. And my shoulders, and my lower back, and my feet. And my forehead. I risked some soup and some tea and decided the kind of solitude in nature that only a billion dollar fortune could buy was exactly what I needed.

I texted my sisters to let them know that they were indeed going to be aunts. Kiara responded right away. Kaleigh was probably out doing sporty things and would get back to me later. They grow up so fast. I texted my husband to let him know that I was turning off my phone. He could get me through Holger and the house phone if he needed to. Then I found the cheesiest sitcom that I'd been meaning to watch and escaped into bliss. I smiled when I saw Michael walking across the pool deck, the aqua-green and white lights reflecting all around him. It was a full suit and tie type day. His hair was down though. He looked so good.

"Hi."

"You look happy," he said as he leaned over and kissed my lips.

"I am happy. I'm pretending."

"Oh? What are we pretending?"

"That today didn't happen. That I don't have to scramble to find a new assistant before we leave for Miami. And I'm pretending two dozen more wedding gifts that we need to write thank-you notes for didn't show up today while we were at work. And I'm definitely pretending that almost my entire family and almost all of my friends didn't find out that I'm pregnant from a shitty website."

"If it makes you feel any better, they weren't even after us."

"They weren't?"

"Nope. Sylvie Jordan sees Dr. Zelner too and she had an appointment right after us. But she's eight months along and has a movie coming out soon. Her people tipped them off. They just happened to catch us first."

"How do you know all this? This isn't like you." Michael was just as annoyed with the unwanted media coverage, if you could call it that, but he usually ignored it and told me to do the same. This wasn't like him at all.

"I made a call."

"Really?"

"There's catching us walking down the street and there's catching us coming out of doctor's appointments. They can at least give us until you start showing. When it's not just speculation."

I slid down the cushions and pulled up the skirt of my dress. I had a bit of a tummy, but I was mostly tits and ass and really big thighs. "I can't see past my boobs, but am I showing now?"

"I think there's a little something there, yeah." I shivered as he gently ran his fingers over my belly. He kissed me a few times, trailing his lips all over my skin. My fingers slipped into his soft hair and swept it away from his face. "Hey babies."

"Baybay One and BayBay A. Individuals of equal importance."

"God, twins really are a handful. I have to have more conversations with your dad, don't I?"

"Oh yeah."

"Okay then. Well, Babies A and One, cover your ears. I'm gonna make out with your mom."

"Are you?"

"Oh yeah." He climbed back up the cabana seat, caging me between his arms. "We had an appointment last night. I think now is as good a time as any to make up for it."

"Go slow," I said with a little pout. "I'm achy and so, so fragile."

"Then I better start slow, huh?"

"Yeah."

And go slow he did. He ditched his tie first. And then his jacket and his dress shirt. It was quite the show, watching him peel away the skintight undershirt. I was ready. I had been ready since the moment he joined me on the cushions, but seeing my name on his chest, that made me ache. My pussy clenched on itself, suddenly desperate for something only he could give me. He saw how impatient I was getting, even though I asked for him to go slow. He reached for the hem on my maxi dress and together we shimmied it up the length of my body. My bra was next. I sat up so he could pull it all the way off.

"Are they sensitive?" he asked.

"Yes," I nearly moaned as he gently pushed them together. He sucked each tip, pulling them to an almost painful point, but I held on to him, digging my fingers into his hair. No way I wanted him to stop. I came, writhing against him, saying his name, urging him to keep going. His erection hard against my hip.

When neither of us could stand it anymore, he moved to my neck. Started with a kiss, soft but sweet with that lazy but firm drag of his tongue across my skin. It turned to sucking, almost hard enough to leave a mark. I reached for him, groping the crotch of his pants. His belt slipped free in my hands and together we pulled off his pants and his boxer briefs and then my husband was truly all mine. He let me stroke him a few times. Let me enjoy the feeling, the thickness of him between my fingers then he was on top of me again, kissing and sucking at my shoulder and neck. His hand spread my thick thighs apart. All the woman he'd ever need, he'd told me once. I felt myself soaking even more as he worked his fingers inside of me. It had to be the hormones, the increase of everything, but it had never felt so good.

"This isn't gonna end up online tomorrow, is it?" I asked with a giggle that melted into a sob as he positioned himself to rub his hard cock along my clit. "Are there drones flying through the canyon?"

"No, baby. And if there are, you know I'll handle it." Of course he would. He always did.

Michael sank himself inside my pussy, all the way, nice and deep, and I thought I would cry when he pulled back and then pushed himself in. He did it again and again.

This was better than make believe, more than compensated for the gossip rags and the misinformed ex-assistants and the things I wanted to keep private until I had time to fully process them. This was everything. The way his body moved over me, inside of me, the way I couldn't stop saying his name. The sweat, both of ours, mixing on my chest as I wrapped my legs around him and pulled him closer, begged him, always begged him to fuck me harder.

I knew I'd need to mentally check out for a few days. Ignore everything that was going on around us. But this, the love we made, it was real and I was never letting it go. I came twice more, a big explosive orgasm as he ground his hips against mine and another long series of blinding tremors as he fucked me to his finish.

When he couldn't support his own exhausted weight anymore, he collapsed beside me on the cabana seats.

"Inside," I huffed. "We might have to do that again when we go inside."

"I might have to rethink that Viagra prescription."

"Yeah right. Fuck around, leave me with two kids and Holger? I'll dig you up and kill you myself."

Michael laughed, then pulled me closer, wrapping his arms around me. Maybe one more time before we went inside, I told myself. That would do the trick.

Chapter Six

I got to play pretend for another twenty-four hours. Thanks to Michael and his magical dick down, I was feeling loose and relaxed enough to share a few bites of his dinner, this delicious Italian dish Holger put together. I was half dead, hurling with heartburn up to my eyebrows half the night. My fabulous husband got up and made me this peppermint concoction he and Holger had looked up after my first sonogram. The next morning, I was in no mood to get dressed and go to work. I texted Daniella, letting her know I wouldn't be in.

Dying. Actually dying. Pray for me. Pray for the children.

Are you really dying, like in the ER or ...?

Being dramatic. Morning sickness is really all day and all night sickness and it's fucking bullshit.

I don't doubt it. Future Adopters of America Unite. Lay down and call me when you're up to it. We've got resumes to review.
Also A Debbie Newman from Notable Moments called and left a message with a kind of bizarre congratulations and a request for a meeting.

I stared at the text, trying to think what they could possibly have in mind. We'd been trying to get one of our Millennial lines picked up by the greeting card giant for almost a year, but other than their Twitter account exchanging tweets with our Twitter account, they kind of acted like we didn't exist.

I'll call her back, I offered but Daniella had it covered.

You rest. I'll call her. It could be nothing.

She was right. We were the little guys. They could be asking us for something silly. I thanked her again for being the best friend/business partner ever, then burrowed back under my sheets.

Turns out Notable Moments actually wanted something. Something big. Thanks to WeNeedEnoughMaterialfor24hoursofClickbait.com, someone in their office had picked up that I was pregnant. Well really, it was thanks to Lili and her awesome social media-ing that we were even on their radar, but now that they knew I was pregnant, they wanted to do a partnership with K&D. I had no idea, but Notable Moments had a baby line, like baby clothes and accessories that went with their modern home stationery collection. At first it made no sense to me. When I think stationery, I don't think onesies, but the patterns actually transferred nicely.

They wanted us to partner with them on a line of cards, babywear and maternity graphic tees for today's mom and they wanted me to be the face of the line. I politely asked if I could think about that part. I wasn't sure if I even wanted to do it. I liked working behind the scenes, and I wanted to talk to Michael about it. Not that he would have tried to stop me, but we were a team now and teams talk. We agreed to regroup in a few weeks. I'd show them some design ideas and they'd show up with some contracts and some real money. I still felt like shit, but the prospect of doing something at work that actually let me focus on the babies and my own pregnancy got me all energized again.

I got a good bit done, but had to pause to see what fruit best resembled the current size of A and One. This was my life now. Work and then googling baby stuff. I stayed away from the scary shit, but found like twenty really cool videos on home births. No way in hell that was happening, though I could see Holger being up for the challenge, but they were still really fascinating to watch. Michael came home when I was deep in a youtube playlist. I looked up when Patch ran to meet him and Penny in the kitchen.

"Our babies are the size of kumquats." I wanted to talk to him more about the Noteable Moments deal, but this was more pressing.

"Full of vitamin C." He stepped down into the living room, then leaned over the back of the couch to kiss me. He tasted minty. That meant face to face meetings all day.

"We need names," I declared.

"Okay. Already? We have some time."

"Yeah, I suppose we have about six months and some change, but I want to decide. Besides I want monogrammed everything. Initials everywhere. I gotta start placing orders. And who knows, you might want more tattoos."

"Forward thinking. I like that," he said absentmindedly touching his chest. He turned like he was going to walk out of the room but I wasn't done yet. "We doing Ks or Ms? Or you wanna start something new with Bs? Get a little alliteration going."

He turned around and thought for a moment while he pulled out his hair tie and shook his ponytail loose. "Think Bs sound good. Let's brainstorm and maybe our HoneyDate this weekend, we can dine in and have a little name selection game."

"You still want to do HoneyDates?"

"You don't? I thought it was a great idea. I still do. You're still crazy in love with me right? 'Cause I still love you. I miss you all day long," he teased.

"I am and I do. I miss you like crazy," I sang the last bit. "I just kinda ruined everything we had on our list."

"You didn't ruin anything. We readjust, that's all baby." He came back over to the couch and sat down beside me. "It'll go fast, but six months is still a long time. I don't want you to stress yourself out. There's plenty of time to just enjoy us."

"There is no us, Michael. Only Zuul."

"That was creepy as fuck. I'm going to hit the head and then I have to make some calls. Tame Ardmenson got arrested last night."

"Again?" The Flames starting guard was nasty on the court and a complete fucking idiot off it. He'd never been charged with anything, but he was couldn't keep his ass out of trouble during the off-season. Luckily he was white, so he usually got scooped up and not gunned down in the street.

"Yeah," Michael said, scrubbing the back of his neck. "He trashed a VIP section at some club in Dallas. I think he already got someone to spring him from the clink, but I have to talk to Rick and Bata tonight. We gotta release him."

Michael had come into possession of The Flames after the previous owner, who was now awaiting trial, had literally hired a hitman to kill a guy who owed him thousands in gambling debts. Michael, the head coach, the general manager and ninety-nine percent of the players had busted their asses to bring a wholesome family vibe back to the city and team. Ardmenson was kind of fucking that up for them."Let me make a call and then Operation Name Our Children is on."

"Deal. I'm sorry this is happening."

"Me too."

I watched my husband as he walked down the hallway toward one of the spare bathrooms, thinking over what he had just said. I had to take care of myself, that was for sure, but he was right. A lot could happen in six months and while I was busy playing walking incubator, I still had a life to live. And Valentine designs to stop ignoring.

The next morning, I decided to suck it up and go back into the office, after my appointment with Dr. Fuckface Cheerful Pants. The girls were happy to see me and Patch, which just made me feel worse.

"I feel awful bailing on you guys so much," I told Daniella as we made ourselves comfortable on the couch with our laptops. "But I got some stuff done, if that counts."

"Dude. Please do not worry about it . You're pregnant. Two times. I can't even imagine what that's like."

"Please tell me if you want me to shut up about it at any point." In all seriousness, Daniella had talked to me and Lili about certain things that just didn't apply to her and things I'd never considered when it came to being a trans woman. I knew the burn of having friends who had no clue what it was like to be black. I didn't want to be that asshole.

"Oh no, trust me. My mom's story of our births scared the living shit out of me."

"For real," Lili added from across the room. She made quite the face.

Daniella laughed. "She was in labor with me for like a million hours. A million plus five with that one. I get to play with super cute babies I don't really have to be responsible for and it gives me an excuse to shop. And when it's mom time for me, I'll have my best friend to give me all kinds of advice." She leaned over and put her head on my shoulder then gave my leg a little squeeze.

"See if I screw them up first."

"Shut up. You're gonna be great at it. Also it's been a nice distraction. I think Duke is seeing someone."

"Oh no."

"Oh yeah. It'll be fine. Just give me like a calendar year to get over him and everything will be a'okay."

If there were a way I could have forced the two of them into a room and screamed at them until they could see they belonged together, I would have. But grown folks gonna grown folk and there was nothing I could do about it. Daniella was a hopeless romantic, but not in the I-secretly-love it-when-my-friends-fuck-with-my-love-life holiday movie sort of way. I just had to let it go.

"Okay," she said, pretending to crack her knuckles. "Let's see what we got."

In just a couple days, fifty resumes had come in. Some from our online listings and some from Ruben and other friends. It was a lot to go through. It hurt my head just to think about it. I was thinking about my tummy neighbors and the precious lining of my esophagus. My husband. I couldn't stop thinking about Michael and all the HoneyDates we had to cross off our list by default, and the ones we could salvage. A million other things that had nothing to do with finding a new assistant or touching bases with our freelancers, or taking Notable Moments' money, or finishing my own designs that were due to the printers whether the smell of Jade's shampoo made me want to forget how to inhale or not. Still, we set up ten interviews. That took more than half the day.

"I think you might want to hire your own personal, *personal* assistant too. Someone in Miami," Daniella said when I came back from a trip to the hurl bucket that was all sound and fury signifying nothing because my stomach was empty. I sipped one of the protein shakes Dr. Assface had recommended, turning the idea over in my head.

"Nah, is my honest answer."

"Okay then."

"We need help here. Plus Holger and Vera will be in Miami with me."

"Vera is very organized."

"Oh god, have you heard Michael's Scottish accent?"

"Not yet. Do I really want to?"

I grabbed my phone and hit Michael's number.

"Yes, my darling," he said after one ring.

"You two are killing me," Daniella said, scrunching her nose up at my phone.

"Hey babe. I have you on speaker. Do the accent. I want the girls to hear."

"I'm just steppin' inta a meetin', aye."

"Oh my god. That's horrible!" Daniella squealed.

"More later," Michael said in his normal voice. "Gotta go. Love you."

"Love you, too."

"He didn't do that in front of any actual Scottish people, did he?" Daniella asked.

"Oh no. That would have gotten us banned from the whole country and we want to go back next year." My stomach sank as soon as I said the words. I swallowed the sudden lump in my throat. "Well maybe not next year."

"You'll get back." Daniella said with a warm smile. "And you'll take me with you."

"And me. Jesus Christ," Lili said. "You jerks never take me anywhere."

"What are you talking about? We took you on Faux Spring Break to Mexico," Daniella said.

"Mexico is like two hours from here!"

"We'll take you to Scotland, Lili," I said before a sister fight broke out. "You can come too, Jade."

"I'm good," she said, deadpan. She didn't even look up from her computer. That's why I liked Jade. Laser focus. Which reminded me, I had to try to at least complete one design before I went home. The core of our little business was not going to create itself.

Oh how I took Brittany for granted and oh how I hated interviewing people. I hated asking people interview questions. Daniella was so much better at it than I was. Even back in our HR days, she was good with the one on one and I was better with the mundane paperwork. Or maybe I was just so distracted that I hated having to sit through the interviews, period. I wanted just the right person to magically walk through the door. Like Mary Poppins, but without the life lessons and the singing. We just needed someone who could pick up right where Brittany left off, someone smart with a good sense of humor who didn't mind that Daniella and I were incapable of keeping our personal lives out of the office. Someone who clicked with Lili and didn't annoy Jade.

There was Christa, who was twenty minutes late because she forgot the address. After our brief two on one with her, Jade suggested we follow her uncle's interview tactics and refuse to interview people who couldn't bother to arrive on time. That rule of thumb had merit, but neither of us could be that brutal. Still, Christa was out. Erin, who had this amazing resume she'd created in inDesign was right on time, but reeked of weed so bad I had to take a step back and hold my nose the minute she walked in the door. Daniella cut right to the chase and asked if she was high, which she freely admitted to 'cause you know it was just part of how she was brought up. No big deal. Daniella killed the interview right there for all of our sakes. I was all for recreational good times, but damn there was a time and place and that scent was just too much.

Telvin was terrified of dogs and would not stop looking over at Patch, who in turn took that as his cue to come over and say hello. That was the end of Telvin. No clue why he applied in the first place considering we put "Must Like Dogs. We have one in the office" in the job posting, but whatever. I'd never seen a man hop over a chair so fast in my life. We settled on Hannah. A soft-spoken, soft butch Korean girl Jade had actually recommended. Hannah and Lili had almost identical temperaments, she loved dogs and she asked us a ton of questions that let us both know that she'd actually thought about the job before she drove out to interview. She was also fine with travel and the odd responsibilities of assisting two people who were definitely learning as they went. She was available to start right away.

After that was settled, and Lili got to work setting up Hannah's email and phone, we were back to playing catch up and meeting this deadline for Notable Moments. And lord did I try, but Kiara would not stop sending me links to adorable baby stuff and of course I had to look at all of it. Plus Michael and I were off to Miami in a few days. I had to pack, had to plan, had too much to do and almost no time to do it. Just six and a half more months and then eighteen years after that, and maybe a few decades after that and I'd be able to take a break and breathe.

Chapter Seven

At different points in my life I'd been tired and overwhelmed. But I'd never known the pure suckery of being tired, overwhelmed, underfed and pregnant in Miami humidity during hurricane season. When we arrived in Florida I had just slid into my second trimester. I was free of Dr. Zelner and immediately had my first appointment with Dr. Angelique Prado, who had actually had twins herself and didn't smile at me like she was trying to get me to understand big words. Michael and I toured the swanky hospital where I'd be giving birth and that gave me a little peace of mind, but still, months to go and so, so much to do. I decided to stop thinking about the fact that I actually had to raise two small children when they arrived and focused on just getting to my delivery date, but that barely helped.

The Notable Moments deal was stressing me out. Michael and I talked, and I decided being the face of the line wasn't something I was particularly interested in. For starters, I was far from the spokesperson for our generation. I loved the idea of "the millennial mom" but I was married to a billionaire. Other than our love of sarcasm and feminism, I knew my life and that of the typical twenty/thirty-something mom didn't have all that much in common. Daniella and I brainstormed the idea of having different "real" moms and pregnant ladies model the products. Hopefully the folks at Notable Moments would go for it.

My mom thought turning down the opportunity was a big mistake, but I had to tell her gently to back off. The stress, my god the stress. The more I thought about the project, the more I found myself obsessing over my current gestational situation. There was no such thing as a distraction anymore. I had babies, moms, pregnancy, maternity wear and accessories on the brain twenty-four hours a day. It got to the point where I actually looked forward to the moments where Daniella needed to talk to me about other random business things. I started to live for the breaks in my day when I had to check in with our freelancers and approve designs for actual holidays.

Even when Michael and I managed to squeeze in a HoneyDate, we would only make it maybe five minutes without one of us bringing up how I was feeling or the way my body was changing. I felt like a complete dick because Michael being Michael, he couldn't help but be honest about his excitement. He was in full dad mode and sort of in awe of having me as his wife and making him a father. I couldn't tell him that I didn't want to talk about the babies being the size of a peach.

Everyone around me was in some kind of mode actually. Kaleigh and Kiara were so psyched to be aunts to the twins. Kaleigh wanted two boys and Kiara sometimes wanted two girls, but also thought a girl and a boy would be a nice addition to the family. Michael and I set up accounts for them that they were both very responsible with but that didn't stop them from buying me tons of baby-related things and having them overnighted to the house. Some of the stuff joined the pile of wedding gifts I'd insisted we ignore. My parents, of course, were excited and worried, but more so excited. They got to be the grandparents. They weren't responsible for stuff like teaching my kids how to walk and talk and how to use a fork and avoid peer pressure.

And then the girls. Daniella and Lili were over the moon. Aunties By Proxy, as they liked to call themselves, so much so that they asked me to design them t-shirts whenever I got a chance. I added that to my to-do list. And even though Daniella and Lili were three thousand miles away, Zia and my friend Asia were right here in Miami with their own set of comments and inquiries. Now that I was showing and knew what parts of the city to avoid so photogs wouldn't catch my newly adopted Fuck All This Shit face, Asia was nice enough to have us over to her house for lunch one rainy Friday when I was feeling particularly cranky.

Thanks to her husband's position as a starter for the Flames, they had their own absurdly large house and a cook and hired help to lend a hand with their three little ones. Tyrie and Persia were already back in school, but her thirteen-month old, Tika, joined us for our meal. There was no escape for me. Babies everywhere.

I tried to make myself comfortable. My ass felt too big for every chair.

"I have to admit, I'm happy for selfish reasons," Asia laughed. I watched her as she gingerly held Tika's chubby fists and helped the baby take clumsy steps around the table. "We might get you here year around."

"Oh no," I groaned. "Please don't say that."

"You got a few years, maybe. But you're gonna want to be here for the season and then when they get old enough, they make friends. We tried to head back to Texas last summer and Tyrie was not having it. His little homies had plans and we had to stay right here."

"Please don't tell me that. Tell me I'm in charge. Tell me I can make my marriage work over the phone."

"Girl, good luck. And just watch, you're gonna sign those birth certificates and every private preschool in Dade county will start hitting you up before the ink dries. They're gonna want those Bradbury billionaires on their roll call."

I groaned again and rubbed my stomach. "But it's so humid here. So wet."

"It's hot in L.A. too," Zia laughed.

"Not like this. Dear god, not like this. Michael needed to buy a team somewhere cooler."

"Too late. We're keeping you. Just claim that residency and make yourself comfortable," Asia laughed.

"Ugh, that reminds me. I haven't even changed my name on my license yet."

"You should get on that, Mrs. Bradbury," Zia said.

I rolled my eyes and tried a bite of the turkey burger Elena, their cook, had prepared for me. That was all I'd been craving recently, ground turkey and grapes.

"Have you picked out names yet?" Zia asked.

"We have."

"Well?"

I'd liked to pretend that Michael and I agonized over the names but we didn't. Once we settled on Bs it was pretty easy to agree on options we were both very happy with.

"Buck and Blaze. Those feel gender neutral. I'm kidding. Brayden, no matter what for Baby One, and Bryan for Baby A if it's a boy or Bethany if it's a girl. Stereo Speaker and Mayor McCheese also made the shortlist, but we thought maybe those names might cause some problems."

"I don't know," Zia said. "Stereo Speaker is growing on me."

"Don't you even think about it," Asia laughed and Tika joined in with her own giggle as she bounced on her wobbly knees. "My children can't associate with anyone named after any sort of household appliance."

"Don't worry. My mama would fly down here and change the birth certificates herself," I replied as my phone chirped in my bag. It was Daniella's text alert. I was tempted not to look at it, but it was a work day.

Just emailed with Deb. CC'd you. We're on for Monday. You good to go, sexy mama?

I smiled at my phone, but suddenly wanted to throw it in Asia's pool. I didn't have words for what I was feeling, but it felt like something close to my body's early warning system going off. Still, duty called.

"Sorry. It's Daniella," I said as I started texting back.

I will be. I added the smiley face emoji with the biggest grin. I worked best under pressure. I'd made great progress but the final touches on the Notable Moments presentation would definitely be handled in the eleventh hour, Sunday night after I'd spent part of the weekend pretending that I didn't have a responsible life to lead or a business to help run or people to not disappoint. I knew I should've been tinkering with it right then, but I had to give myself at least an hour or so to enjoy my lunch with my friends.

I scooted to the end of my chair and held out my hands for Tika. "May I?" I asked Asia.

"Oh my god. Please." Asia handed off Tika and her soft, chubby little fists, then flopped down in her chair with a deep sigh.

"I'm stupid to think I can do two at once, aren't I?" I said as Tika scrutinized my face. When I realized her look of confusion was matching mine, I smiled and cooed at her and made her laugh. No reason to bring her down with me.

"Oh you'll be fine. Trust me. It feels terrifying now, but once they show up you just go. You know what I mean?"

"I've heard you love them so much you want to make sure they're clean and fed. Stuff like that." I looked at Zia and she winked at me. I knew she was right. I loved my little nuggets already, but that day it was a little hard to see the big picture. Whether or not I liked it though, the big picture was going to show up in just a few short months.

Sunday night snuck up on me like a damn bandit. Michael had a full week ahead of him. Training camp was starting and he still had to keep up with his usual business junk. Our HoneyDate that weekend involved Michael giving me a foot massage. It was the most romantic shit he had ever done for me. I'd finished my presentation for Notable Moments. I knew there was more I could do. More tweaks, maybe a little more polish, but I just couldn't look at the designs anymore. Michael proofread the copy for me after dinner and then I declared myself free to relax for the next nine hours.

I was trying to make myself comfortable in bed so we could snuggle and watch a movie. Patch was sitting patiently on the floor, waiting for me to get my shit together so he could set up shop on my side of the bed. He was fascinated by my belly, and sick to shit of having to readjust every time I couldn't find my perfect spot. Just as I patted the bed and signaled for him to jump up, Michael's business cell started break dancing on his night stand.

"Babe!" I called for him, just as he came striding out of the bathroom. His shirt was off, but he was still wearing his jeans. He scowled at the screen then hit accept. I reached over then and quickly made sure my own phone was plugged into its charger.

"Hey, Nick. Yeah, it's fine. What's going on?" I couldn't make out what the person on the other end was saying, but if I had to guess, it was Nick Yang. No freaking clue why he was calling. "Hey, hey, no man. It's okay. It's okay. What's going on?"

Michael sat on the bed and reached over and rubbed my stomach through our bedspread. I could barely hear Nick on the other end, but he was loud enough that I could hear the frantic tone in his voice.

"Tonight?!" Michael said. More mumbling. Still frantic. "Okay. Okay. I'll be out there in the morning. Okay. No, it's okay." Michael let out a shaky laugh. "I understand. I have a mother too. It'll be fine. I'll see you." He laughed for real this time. "I promise. I won't tell the guys. Yeah. Hide your luggage if you can and I'll see you in the morning."

Michael flopped on his back beside me, then tossed his phone. It bounced twice, then hit Penny in the belly. Her head snapped up. "Sorry, girl."

"Was that Nick Yang?" They had scooped up the rookie point guard from UCLA in round two of the draft. Michael and the coaching staff had high hopes for him, but clearly something was up.

"Yes. It was Nick. I have to go to Seattle tonight."

"What? Why?" Penny whipped her head around and looked at me. It would have been hilarious if I wasn't suddenly super bummed out. Michael rubbed her side, then grabbed his phone again. He started texting.

"Nick's mom saw everything with Ardmenson and now she'd freaking out. She doesn't want him to leave for camp."

"He's like twenty-three, isn't he? And like a professional basketball player now. He can leave the house after dark, right?" Michael often reassured the parents of rookies that their kids were in good hands with the Flames, but this sounded a little extreme.

"I get it, kind of. He's a really good kid. Total straight edge. Like bible study and shit, and he actually organized study groups and tutoring sessions for his college teammates at UCLA so their grades would be legit. Very good family. Very concerned mother. He was too embarrassed to say anything about it."

"Okay, now I feel bad. He does sound like a good guy. And I don't blame Mom. Some of these professional players are a little out of control. Ardmenson isn't the only one. I can understand her being afraid that he's going to get mixed up in some crazy shit."

"His mom loves me though. Apparently I'm the only one who can convince her that this is the right move for her son."

"How are you going to do that?"

"I don't know. For Nick's sake, I hope it doesn't mean buying her a house down here."

"Eeyikes. Yeah."

Michael started moving around the room, sighing again, louder than I'd like. That was the exhausted and frustrated sigh. The why-the-fuck-did-I-buy-a-basketball-team sigh.

"Baby. Come here." I held out my hand and then pulled him closer when he came around to my side of the bed. Patch was not impressed, but he didn't have to move. I reached up and touched the stubble growing in on my husband's cheeks. "I think it's pretty sweet that he trusts you this much, though. You must be a pretty great guy."

"I need to be more of an asshole, huh?"

"Maybe. Just a little bit. I'm gonna let this one slide, but I think the more pregnant I get, the less running off in the middle of the night I'm gonna let you do."

"Shit. I'm sorry. Are you gonna be okay?"

"Yeah, of course. I'll be fine."

"I'll be back tomorrow night. I'm going to take PJ and we'll just grab him and go."

"The old snatch and grab."

"You know it."

"I love you."

Michael leaned forward and kissed me gently on the lips. "I love you too."

I put on some crap TV and stayed awake while Michael got dressed and ready to leave. I was tempted to walk him to the door when Emmanuel brought the car around, but it wasn't happening. I couldn't get up. I hadn't the will. I kissed him goodbye and told him I'd be looking forward to his text in the morning. I hated sleeping without him, but I knew I could manage one night.

I was up all fucking night. I knew there was no magic to keeping food down. Even my favorite cravings betrayed me on a pretty regular basis. I had plenty of nights like this before, but Michael had been there to hold my hair and soothe me back to sleep. The second I woke up the next morning though, I knew something was wrong. Holger had just walked into the room, carrying the laundry.

"Good afternoon, Mrs.," he said.

"Uh fuck, what time is it?" I groaned. I still felt like crap. I rolled, trying to sit up and rubbed my stomach.

"It's one thirty."

"What? Fuck. Fuck! I missed my call." I looked over at my nightstand and my phone was gone. I started frantically patting around the sheets. "Fuck, my phone. Where's my phone? Shit! I think I left it in the bathroom." Holger took off for the bathroom door and came back a few seconds later with my almost dead cell phone. I had a ton of missed calls and voicemails and texts. All from Daniella and Lili. There was one check-in text from Michael wishing me luck with the presentation and telling me he'd call me as soon as he landed and dropped Nick at his hotel. "I tried to wake you earlier but I didn't think I should disturb you," Holger said.

"No, you're fine. I fucked up." I could feel Holger's worried gaze on me as I hit Daniella's number. She answered right away.

"Kay?! Are you okay? What happened?"

"I'm fine. I'm sorry. Michael had to take an emergency trip and I was up all night puking."

"Did you go with him?"

"No, no. I'm home. I was just dead after it finally stopped and I didn't have my phone near me."

"Oh. Okay. I called the house phone after I got off the call, but Vera said you were out cold." Shit. I knew that tone, but it had never been directed at me.

"Fuck, she should have woken me up." But Vera was not responsible for my schedule. She was on house and dog duty. It wasn't her fault that I'd massively fucked up.

"Well, we were done by then anyway, so it wouldn't have mattered."

"Shit, I'm sorry. What happened? Did we lose the account?"

"No, we're good to go. We still have to talk money some more, but I had a few of the designs you'd already showed me—" I wanted to puke all over again. Those designs were very rough. "They loved them, thank god, but they still want to talk to you."

"I'll call them right now. Uhh fuck, who should I ask for?" Daniella had been handling the actual business side of things. She'd set up the call.

"Debbie Newman, she runs the baby line, and Patsy Hargreaves, the CEO."

"Dude. I'm so fucking sorry."

"It's okay." Her voice softened. "I'm just glad you're okay."

"I'm fine. Let me call them. I'll call you back."

"Okay."

I hit end and then shimmied to the edge the bed. Holger held out his hand to help me up. Which was a smart move, 'cause my head instantly started spinning and I teetered a little to the left.

"I'm going to have to insist that you get back in bed."

"I'm not gonna fight you on this." I sat right back down.

"I'm bringing you some tea and some water and as soon as your call is finished, we're calling Dr. Prado. No arguments."

"Sounds good. Can you hand me my laptop?" It was fully charged and safely stored on the bottom shelf of my nightstand. Holger passed it to me and then helped me get settled. Before I could even think to ask, he grabbed one of the portable charges Michael kept stashed on his side of the bed, then rushed out of the room. It took me a few minutes to get my bearings, but after a few calming breaths I fixed my voice and hit send on the number Daniella had provided. Patsy was gone for the day, but I was able to get Debbie on the phone.

"I don't think I can express how embarrassed I am. Women harvest crops and work the mills when they're way more pregnant than I am now and—"

"Kayla, please. It wouldn't make much sense for me to push products to pregnant women and busy parents if I had no empathy for what you're going through. My son was two weeks late and let me tell you, the joys of an emergency c-section. One missed meeting when you're dealing with twins is not enough to get us to go back on our proposal."

"Thank you so much. I'd love to send you the rest of the designs," I said. "I can shoot them over now if you don't mind."

"Absolutely. Show me what you got."

Debbie skipped an internal meeting to go through each item with me, giving me notes and showering me with praise for the more humorous onesies and cards. Her personal favorite was a little t-shirt that said "Puréed, Not Stirred" with a smiling carrot holding hands with a winking spoon below it. She let me apologize a few more times and let me know that they'd have an offer over by the end of the week.

I called Daniella as soon as we were done, but she didn't answer. She sent me a text right away though.

On the phone with Jade and the rep from FedEx. Call you back in a sec.

A sec turned into three hours, but she couldn't talk long. She and Lili were meeting their parents for dinner. I knew she wouldn't be mad at me forever, but I also knew that I had really fucked up.

Guilt and restlessness led me to convincing Holger that he should help me assemble the two cribs that had already been gifted to us. After we finished, I asked as politely as I could to be left alone. We'd checked in with the doctor and I'd managed to keep down most of my dinner and the small snack he prepared for me. After I promised him that I would keep sipping on my water, he felt comfortable giving me some space.

That's where Michael found me some hours later, sitting on the floor of our de facto nursery, our new 64-piece tool kit splayed out on the floor beside me. I'd settled on the flat head screwdriver, twisting the smooth blunt end between my fingers, just focusing on the way my skin gave around the metal, thinking about how much of a mess I'd made.

"Hey," Michael said cautiously as he entered the room.

I looked up, then back down at my hands. I couldn't see his face anyway. The hallway light was casting him in total shadow.

"Hey."

He squatted beside me and stroked my hair. "Holger told me it was a rough day. How are you feeling?"

"Not great." His touch moved to my forehead then eased down my cheek. "I really let Daniella down. I don't think I've ever disappointed her before. It feels awful."

"I lost Steven three million dollars once."

"Really?"

"Yep. Some investments are just bad, but I learned a valuable lesson and our friendship survived. And I don't even like him as much as you and Daniella like each other. Talk to her. Let her say what she needs to say. You two will work it out."

"I don't know what I'm doing." I looked up at him as a fat tear ran down my cheek. "I think she just won us our first huge piece of business and all I can think about are these kids. They aren't even here yet and they are all I can think about. It's scaring me."

Michael's thumb brushed my tears away. He kissed my lips.

"I was thinking about you the whole time I was gone. I was standing there in Mrs. Yang's living room trying to explain to her that Nick was smart enough to keep his personal life a hundred miles away from the backseat of a cop car, and I was just picturing your face," he said with an unapologetic shrug. "I'm shifting all this money around, making sure that I'm making all the right moves for my sites, the apps, the team, but every single second my mind is on you. It is scary. The stakes is high." I laughed as his mustache lifted a bit at the corner.

"But we do this together, right?" he said. "We get through this together. If it becomes too much, you have me and I have you. And when they are old enough to return the favor, if we do this whole parent thing well enough, Brayden and Bethany will be there for us too."

"You want girls, don't you?"

"There are so many men in my professional life, it only seems fitting that my home be filled with amazing women." I could only shake my head and wipe my face. "I desperately need a shower. Would my beautiful, amazing, smart, kind, caring wife care to join me?"

"Yeah, I guess." Michael chuckled a little as he helped me up.

We said our goodnights to Vera and Holger, then made our way to the bedroom. I let Michael undress me and then got under the hot spray of our dual head shower as he got rid of his own clothes. The minute I saw his naked body, that large and now healed tattoo of my name sprawled across half his chest and his semi-hard erection, I wanted him to fuck me. But there was no way that was happening in the shower, not standing up, my body wasn't having it. After we toweled off and lotioned up though, I let Michael spoon me between our soft sheets and dropped the oh so subtle hints that I wanted him inside of me.

"I want you to fuck me," I whispered to him in the dim light of our bedroom. He didn't say a word, just moved closer and started kissing on my shoulder as his hand slid up to my sensitive breasts. His cock was already hard against my ass. My pussy was already wet. I reached back and guided him in the general direction of where I wanted him to be. My ass was too fat and my belly too round to put him in myself, but my husband knew what he was doing, he knew the drill, knew exactly how I liked it.

I leaned forward just a little, moaning his name as he pushed his way between my swollen, wet lips. I squeezed my eyes closed, savoring the even motion of his hips, the gentle push and pull that became more frantic as my hormone-riddled lust became too much for me and I started to beg. I lost myself, biting my lip nearly raw to keep from screaming as his hand smoothed over my tender skin and captured my clit. I came, hard, gasping for air as I pushed myself back against him. I wanted him as deep as he could go. That orgasm gave me the boost I needed to climb on top of him so we could do it all over again.

This second round, somehow it was better, my hands bracing the wall above our headboard as he sucked my nipples into his mouth. I cried out this time, his name mixed with profanities as I clenched down around him. He wasn't far behind, gripping my lower back with his strong hands as he filled me with every last drop. After, after I drank a little water and after he cleaned away the traces of our lovemaking from between my thighs, we lay there together, his arms around my shoulders and my head resting on that new ink.

"I have to go to L.A," I told him. "I have to make things right with Daniella in person."

"Do you want me to go with you?"

My eyes started welling up again. Michael was up to his eyebrows with his own shit. He'd just spent twenty-four hours traveling just to protect the interests of his team and I knew he'd pack right back up and accompany me on another six thousand mile trek.

"I don't deserve you."

"You deserve everything your heart desires."

"As much as I'd love you to, I think I have to handle this alone."

"If you change your mind..."

"I know, babe. You got me."

"Always."

Chapter Eight

I thought I was going to get away with a solo trip to Los Angeles, but Holger, of all people, wasn't having it. He didn't say as much to me, but Michael let it slip that my little episode had really scared Holger. The secondhand account worried Michael too, but he trusted me to let him know when I wasn't up to something. I could manage a cross-country flight alone, but I agreed to let Holger tag along, just in case. We got in Wednesday night. It was strange staying in the Malibu house without Michael, but I FaceTimed with him and the puppies before bed.

The next morning, I called the girls and took their breakfast orders. It's always better to show up with food. Daniella was still a little tense with me, but I figured she didn't hate me too much when she asked for a breakfast sandwich and an iced coffee instead of telling me to shove my food-related bribes up my ass. PJ delivered Holger and I to the office a little before ten a.m., thanks to that glorious L.A. traffic.

"I have food," I said sheepishly as Holger held open the door for me. Daniella looked up and flashed me a half smile.

"Whoa," Lili said as she rushed over to take the coffees out of my hands. Daniella wasn't far behind. She took the breakfast sandwiches from Holger. Or tried to anyway.

"Nonsense. I am here to serve. Come ladies, gather round." Lili and Hannah joined him on the couch. Even Jade got with the program and came over and grabbed a seat in the armchair.

"Hey," I said to Daniella.

"Hey."

"Can we go outside and talk?"

"Of course." She grabbed her iced coffee and followed me outside. I knocked on the window of the SUV and asked PJ to pop the trunk.

"Thanks," I said as I lifted the tailgate. "PJ, you can go for a walk if you want."

"No, I can't."

"Fair enough. Ear muffs, then." PJ just shook his head and went back to looking out the window.

"I forget that he can talk sometimes," Daniella whispered as we both climbed up and took a seat in the back of the Suburban.

"Me too." I took a deep breath and did my best to hold off with the crying, I knew it wouldn't last very long. "I'm really sorry. I know I fucked up really bad and I don't think I can make it right."

"Oh, Kay." Daniella sighed and let her head fall on my shoulder.

"I know you're mad at me and I feel like it's just going to get worse."

"What makes you say that?"

"'Cause I don't know that it won't happen again. I feel like I can't make promises anymore because my life isn't just mine anymore." And then the waterworks started. I reached for the pack of tissues I had in the pocket of my cardigan.

"Yeah, but I understand what happened. It's pretty freaking understandable. I wasn't—I was mad, but I think it was for different reasons at first than you're thinking. I was mad that you made me worry. I thought you were dead. And then I was worried about the babies and then you again. And then I was super pissed because I felt like a complete asshole during that meeting."

"Debbie made it sound like you crushed it though."

"Yeah, and that was pure luck. I have no idea what would have happened if you and I weren't at least a little on the same page, if you hadn't sent me some of the early designs. I felt like a complete jackass. It ended well, but I definitely panicked in the beginning. I had no clue if they would just yank the offer. I don't know. I take this shit seriously and then when I found out that you'd just overslept—okay, I was mad at you. And now I feel worse because it is completely understandable. I mean look at you."

We both looked down at my stomach. I wasn't bursting at the seams, but it was pretty fucking obvious that I was pregnant. Daniella sighed and rocked forward a bit. "I am happy for you. You and Michael have pulled together this amazing life and now twins? It's crazy. This time three years ago, you and me were trying to distract ourselves from our boring as fuck jobs by plotting how to get Gordo to ask John out at the Halloween party. That was as excited as it got."

"That was pretty fun, though."

"It was and even more fun when John turned out to be a complete tool and Gordo couldn't shake him." We both laughed. Our days in corporate human resources seemed a world away. "I don't know, I guess I never thought that *you* dating someone would have such an impact on my life. And then when you were M.I.A., I just had this moment of what the fuck am I doing? Duke and I are done for good. I swear this time. And you and Michael are starting this next huge chapter and—"

"And you don't know if you want to be a part of this?"

"I don't know if *you* do."

Even fatter tears ran down my cheeks. This was the conversation I didn't want to have. This was what I wanted to avoid. "I didn't think this through, any of this. I didn't want to freeload off Michael and I'm good at graphic design. I thought it would be a great idea to start this company and of course Michael could make it all happen. He also made this happen." I rubbed my stomach again. "It was all just happening, but I wasn't thinking long term at all. And I dragged you in with me."

"Yeah, well, it wasn't exactly like it took much convincing. I was rushing along on this ride too. Do you want to sell the company?"

"I don't think so, no."

"But you don't know what you want to do?"

"I want to survive this pregnancy with my sanity intact. I want whatever comes next to make you happy."

"You know I'm not attached to all this right?"

I whipped my head around. "What do you mean?"

"This is your baby, dude. I'm glad to be on the team, don't get me wrong, and I am beyond pleased to not be working at Tellett anymore, but I'm not attached to this concept. I mean, I'm a little attached to Queer Qards 'cause you make the bestest cutest designs for that line, but the rest? Eh. Greeting cards aren't my passion."

"So what are you saying?"

"I just want you to keep me in the loop. I knew you were having a rough time, but you are also like the queen of hyperbole."

"I do tend to exaggerate from time to time. You may be right there."

"I've never seen you like this before."

"Do I look that bad?" I teased. I'd actually taken my time getting ready that morning and I'd gotten a decent night's sleep. I looked fabulous.

"No, but you look different. You've changed and I'm not just talking the tummy tenants. I didn't realize you were this exhausted. I don't even know how you finished the proposal on time and finished all the other design shit we have going on."

"And that's why I don't know what to do. I...I want to stay home with them. My mom worked, but she or my grandma was always with us. I don't want some random nanny or Holger—good, god, can you imagine?"

"You'd have these cute babies with the weirdest German accents, living in South Florida." I looked over at her, the shock clear on my face. She'd been thinking about me living there for good too.

"And that is the other thing. Michael and I, we have to stay. Above all this, even all his other projects, the team takes priority. He has to show his face and I have to be there with him. These kids are going to be spoiled as shit, but I don't want to be flying my children back and forth across the country all the time. And before, at least when you and Duke—"

"Yeah, I had excuse to come to Miami all the time."

"Yeah."

"You can still be my excuse though, right?"

"You can use me as an excuse to rack up as many air miles as you like. There are things there that money can buy, but I want to be a good mom."

"You will be, Kay. I know you will."

We sat there for a few moments in silence, listening to the traffic go by on the other side of the hedges.

"Life is weird, huh?"

"It definitely is," Daniella laughed. Then she stood and faced me and let out a deep breath. "Okay. First things first. Let's think about the actual work. Do you still like designing greeting cards?"

"I do."

"Okay. So there's that. Do you want to do this project with Notable Moments? Try not to think about the babies, just for a sec. Does this project still interest you?"

"It does."

"Okay. Then I propose this—we hire an Art Director or something similar. Someone who can create and oversee designs and take some responsibilities off your plate, but you'll still have final say."

"I actually like that idea. Okay, yeah."

"Then I say you take a proper maternity leave. Take a real break. Obviously you can bug us and barge in whenever you like, but take a real break, real time for you and your family. California law gives you twelve weeks, but I think we can bump you up to sixteen because you've really shown some initiative here, Bradbury. You've earned it."

"Thanks, boss."

"But really, take the time you need and then in a year or whatever, we reevaluate. We'll get this Notable Moments thing off the ground and hey, maybe they'll buy us out. We'll make sure Jade and Hannah have somewhere to land if they're still here and then I'll pack up Lili and we'll move on to the next thing. Shit, by then I'll have some real years of operations management under my belt. I can go anywhere!"

I laughed and playfully swung my foot at her. "I think that's a great idea. Get in here." I opened my arms and squeezed Daniella tight as she stepped forward and hugged me. When she pulled away she looked down at my stomach.

"God, what does it feel like?"

"Like my organs are being jammed up in my neck. And I couldn't be happier about it. Here." I took her hand and put it on my stomach.

"That is so crazy. They can hear voices right? Does Michael talk to them?"

"Every day."

"Of course he does. You two make me sick."

I looked up as the door opened and Lili slid out. She walked over to us, biting at the corner of her nail. "Is everything okay? I don't like it when my moms fight."

"Everything is fine," Daniella said.

"I was just about to butt into your sister's business actually. Maybe you can help me."

"Were you really?"

"I was. I think you should work things out with Duke."

"I second that," Lili said. "He's kind of a bonehead, but he really loves you."

"Well, girls. That's gotta be a two-way street now, doesn't it?"

"You saying you don't love him?" I asked, appalled at the blatant fib.

"If I told you how I was really feeling, you'd think I'd lost my damn mind. My breakfast sandwich is getting cold and I'm sure we've all got work to do. Let's get inside, shall we?"

Lili and I exchanged some knowing glances before we followed Daniella into the office.

Five and a Half Months and One Extended Maternity Leave Later

I snapped another picture and sent it to the girls over WhatsApp. Hannah responded to the group chat first.

OMG STEAL THAT BABY!

I laughed and tilted the phone toward Zia so she could read as I responded.

OMG I DON'T WANT TO GO TO JAIL!

Daniella replied next. *So cute! I'm coming to the next shoot for sure. I can't handle it!!*

I rolled my eyes as Jade sent a single thumbs up emoji. At first she was a little reluctant to join in our shenanigans, but she'd finally caved and joined the sisterhood. She liked being a part of the team. So far Daniella's plan had worked out perfectly. We hired Edie Sims-Stokes, who'd been aching to leave her job in advertising. She was the perfect addition to K&D, a smart, funny, forty-something black woman who took the perfect amount of work off my plate. She seemed to be the glue to pull us all together. Edie kept us in line, and with her, the whole concept of Cards by K&D now had a sense of stability that made me feel like it was definitely worth holding on to.

I worked right up to my delivery date, but as it became harder and harder to even use my laptop on my lap, I focused only on my designs and our partnership with Notable Moments. The first "season" of the line had been very well received. Even though I wasn't the face, thanks to the lasting media buzz over our wedding and the announcement that we were having twins, we were able to bring a lot of attention to the products. The huge launch party we had with a mixed guest list of celebrity and regular moms didn't hurt either.

"He has to be the cutest baby you've used yet," Zia murmured.

"I know."

We stood back and watched Debbie and the photographer, Carlos, as they finished up. He shot one more series and then Deb waved me over. Little Oliver's mom came up to the elevated platform in the center of the room and scooped him up off the mat. He'd been so good for the whole shoot. Zia joined them and kept the model and mom company like she did every shoot. She loved working with kids.

"What do you think?" Deb asked. "I think we go it." Carlos clicked on the monitor and showed me the last few dozen shots. We'd done four outfits on Oliver and they all looked great. We had plenty of shots to choose from for the website and more than enough if we wanted to used him for some ads.

"I think it's perfect. I'm good if you guys are," I replied.

"I just want to know when we're going to get your girls in here," Carlos teased for the hundredth time.

"I've been trying," Deb added with her kind smile. Deb was a little quirky, an older white woman from Long Island who had the weirdest laugh, but I liked her. She trusted me and gave me room to work. So far our partnership with Notable Moments was working out just fine.

I scoffed at their not-so-silly request. My daughters were cute as shit, but... "Give us a few more months and I think we can try for Brayden. She loves the camera. Bethany, not so much. She'll sit still for anything, but the moment you start snapping pictures she's like, no, no photographs please. How a four month old figured out how to block her face from the camera, I'll never know."

"Well whenever they're ready, we will gladly use them. And hopefully we can get Mom in on it too," Deb winked at me and then turned to Oscar and his mom to let them know they were free. Carlos announced to the crew that we were wrapped for the day.

I hung around a little while longer, thanked Mora for letting us hire her son, said my goodbyes to Deb and the crew, and promised to catch up with Zia tomorrow, after she turned down my invitation to join us for dinner. She had a date. Emmanuel was waiting for me on his stool perch by the stage door.

"Are you ready, Miss Kayla?"

"Let's do it."

There was some traffic, but we made it back to the house in thirty minutes. Patch ran to meet me at the door.

"Hello?" I called out.

"We're in here," Michael replied, in a sing-song voice. I smiled to myself. I knew what that voice meant. I walked into the living room, right in the middle of tummy time. Michael was lying on the floor with our daughters as they wiggled around. Penny was on the floor between the girls, her head resting on her paws, supervising. I knew this was practice for the development of very important motor skills, but I could not resist. I held out my hands and shuffled across the room right for Bethany, making the most ridiculous noise as I went.

I scooped her up and kissed her right on her chubby little cheeks. "Hello, my sweet baby. Hello. Oh, I missed you."

Michael sat up and held out his hands for her. He knew the drill. It was Brayden's turn. I scooped her off the floor and smothered her was the same adoring kisses. She made the cutest little noise. I was definitely going to keep them both. They were just so cute.

The rest of my pregnancy can only be described as completely ridiculous. Back pain, joint pain, skin pain, organ pain, face pain, balls of my feet pain. Did you know your sternum can bend? 'Cause I didn't. I was as big as a house by the time I went in for my scheduled c-section, but I wouldn't change anything about it. I walked in, convinced I'd never touch my toes again and I came out with two beautiful, healthy baby girls. You could tell right away that they were fraternal. Bethany favored Michael and Brayden looked like a perfect mix of us both. They both came out with full heads of the softest black hair. Brayden had Michael's blue eyes and, as if to ensure that we never mixed them up, Bethany came out with one brown eye and one blue. They were both perfect.

I sunk on the couch with Brayden in my lap. "Did either of them take a bottle?" I asked, pulling my shirt open. "My tits are about to explode."

"Bethany did 'cause she's a team player and she likes to cooperate. Sometimes. But that one?" Michael made a face at Brayden and she wiggled her feet at him.

"She likes it from the source. Don't you, baby girl?" I whipped out my boob and Brayden went right for her dinner. "Oh thank god." I groaned.

"How'd the shoot go?" Michael asked as he stopped Patch from licking Bethany's face. Both he and Penny had been amazing. I was worried at first. As my stomach got bigger, Penny actually became more protective of me, sometimes getting between Michael and I in the most adorable way, but by the time I'd reached six months, Patch was thoroughly weirded out. I couldn't exactly explain what was going on to him in words he'd understand. Michael and I had had the talk, and if either of them couldn't handle being around the babies we'd have to rehome them, but both of the puppies had been so well behaved from the moment we brought the girls home. A little over excited at times, but always sweet and always gentle.

"Shoot was great. Great baby. Great mom. I hope we can use them again."

"That sounds awesome." He glanced at his smart watch. "We can tag team bath time if you want. I gotta call into KTMA for tip off at eight though."

"I absolutely want. You know how much I hate being outnumbered."

"I do."

I sat on the couch, nursing Brayden until she was milk drunk and nearly slipping into a coma, then gave

Bethany a go. Every so often I'd look over at Michael. His beard had a few more gray hairs, some pure white, but he was still just as handsome as the day we met, and somehow more kind, more caring, and more full of love.

He caught me staring at him with a particularly dreamy look in my eye. He shifted Brayden in his arms and joined me on the couch.

"Gimme some sugar," I whispered.

"Oh I'll give you something sweet." He leaned over and kissed me soft and long, right on my lips. We had seven years max before kissing in front of the kids started to gross them out. But for now…I teased the inside of his bottom lip, just a little with my tongue. He returned the favor, offering a little bite.

"Yup," I said with a pitiful groan when I pulled away. "We're definitely having sex tonight. Butt stuff sex, maybe with little Mikey,"

"Does that Little Red Riding Hood costume still fit?"

"Sure does. Tried it on last week while you were at the arena. The slutty Snow White thing kinda fits too."

"Kinda?"

"It's tighter, in the good place."

"Oooh, woman. I love you. And these little punks."

"We love you too. Almost all of the time." I winked at my husband, then I kissed him again.

The End

So much more to come

Hey guys! We've reached the end of Kayla and Michael's journey, but there's still more ahead for their friends and family. Coming in 2017…

NEVER GONNA GIVE YOU UP
(Super Star Scandal #1)

Almost two years after her break up with super producer and pop singer Duke Stone, Daniella Martinez still can't seem to shake her feelings for her ex, a small secret she's kept from everyone including her best friend and her sister. Between the insane tour schedules, producing records for top artists and the groupies —mother of God, the groupies —and the nonstop partying, Daniella knows she's not cut out to accompany Duke through life in the fast lane. But when Duke finds himself in epic drug related legal trouble, it's Daniella his family calls.

Duke knows he and his bandmates have screwed up big time. He's ready to get his life back in order, but what he really wants is a life with his ex-girlfriend, Daniella and he's willing to do whatever it takes to win her back for good. Daniella is more concerned with Duke keeping himself out of trouble than rekindling their shaky romance, but when she realizes that she might actually be the best thing in the world for Duke, Daniella wonders, can he be the man she truly needs?

What More from Rebekah?
Check out chapter one of FIT: #1 in the Fit Trilogy!

FIT
by
REBEKAH WEATHERSPOON

Violet Ryan loves the delicious food she gets to eat on the reality shows she produces for The Food Channel. What she hates is her expanding waistline. Determined to drop the pounds, Violet hatches a plan to kick start a fitness regimen. But when her determination isn't enough to get her through even one intense group class without breaking down into tears, she knows she needs a new approach and possibly a new trainer—one with a lighter touch.

Grant Gibson has always managed to mix business with pleasure, but now this trainer by day, and Dominant by night, is bored. Bored and lonely. Even though he owns one of L.A.'s hottest private gyms, his personal life is sorely lacking. After his last submissive tried to kidnap his dog and the contents of his bank account, he's in no hurry to take a new lover under his wing. Not until the voluptuous Violet falls into his lap.

She may be wary of his unorthodox approach of using sexual gratification as a reward, but even before her initial weigh-in Violet can't seem to stay away from the sexy fitness god. She may have to let Grant show her there's more than one way to get in shape…

This story contains light acts of bondage and a feisty submissive who gives her Dominant a run for his money.

CHAPTER ONE

Day 1

Violet nearly wheezed as she dropped her weights to the ground. She collapsed on all fours, a few drops of sweat beating her to the hard rubber surface. She stretched her hands out, shoulder-width apart. Her knees ached as she raised herself up in a modified push-up. Was it possible to die from push-ups? She didn't know, but part of her wanted it to be true. Sweat ran down her face, between her breasts, and she wanted to die.

Actually, she wanted to kill her friend, Faye. And the people at sharepon.com. Faye had it coming for suggesting they take this all-ladies Pump Fit class together, and sharepon.com deserved a strongly worded letter for offering the class to Faye for free if she brought a friend along to join in the pain. Sure, in reality it was Violet's own fault. She'd spent half their last season on *BBQ Cook-Off* complaining about how much weight she needed to lose, while simultaneously shoving pound after pound of pulled pork into her pie hole.

Faye was a good friend and listened to Violet bitching about the long hours they worked and the high calorie foods they were "forced" to eat on set. Even though Faye seemed to manage the hours and the menus just fine, she listened when Violet confessed that she'd reached her breaking point. Her fat jeans barely buttoned over her stomach the night of the wrap party. It was time to get her body in order.

She'd heard it one hundred and a million times; it takes twenty-one days to create a new habit, and Violet had exactly *twenty-three* days before preproduction started up on their next show for Park Place Productions.

She loved her job as an associate producer. Her company's primary focus was cooking and baking competition shows for The Food Channel. She worked hard and partied even harder, but enough was enough. She had twenty-three days to get on a healthy routine so she could go into the next show with a new diet, a new sleep schedule and, hopefully, a smaller waistline. She envisioned herself taking on this challenge head-on. She'd always been overweight. A chubby kid, turned fat teen, turned fatter adult, but she'd always been somewhat in shape. Pump Fit sounded tough. Still, if she put her mind to it, she could make it through the class. Or so she thought.

"One more minute! Keep going, ladies!" the instructor shouted. Her name was Margaret and even though she was the same height as Violet, she was about ten sizes smaller and carried about seventy-five more pounds of muscle, most of it in the area about the neck and shoulders. Instructor Margaret was from Australia, with an accent so thick her every command would have been hilarious if Violet could find the slightest bit of humor in the situation. Margaret was also a professional Pump Fit competitor. As soon as she offered that bit of information at the start of class, Violet should have run right back to her car.

"Up!" Margaret shouted. "I want twenty burpees! Go!"

Violet struggled to her feet, then dropped back down, extending her legs behind her butt before bringing her knees back up to her chest then springing back up to her feet.

One.

Down again. She could barely breathe. Her lungs burned and that acidic taste, a mixture of burning fat, blood and embarrassment, filled her mouth. Beside her, Faye, with her flat stomach and tight butt, completed burpee three and four. Faye ate her pork too. It wasn't fair.

"Come on, Violet! Keep going! We don't move on until we all finish!"

Right. Great. No pressure there. Violet dropped to the floor one more time, and then again, as Margaret kept screaming.

The buzzer at the front of the room sounded, signaling the end of the timed rotation. Violet had completed six burpees. She'd attempted eight. Margaret frowned at her briefly, but let it go.

"Two hundred meter run! Claire knows the way!" Demon Instructor nodded to a slim redhead, who nodded back then bolted for the open gym door.

"Come on," Faye said, patting Violet's sweaty arm. "You're doing great. Let's go."

Violet kept up as they sprinted down the stairs to the street, but once they hit the hill, the freaking hill that led from the gym plaza to Sunset Boulevard, she started lagging behind. When the second-to-last woman in the class lapped her on the way back, Violet started to cry.

It was gym class all over again. She was the last kid picked. The last kid to finish the mile. The fat-ass who caused the gym teacher's eyebrows to sag down when she even attempted the sit-and-reach. Violet didn't know who she was kidding. She needed more than twenty-three days and her wavering determination. She needed lipo and a miracle.

Violet stopped slow jogging and wiped her face. When she made it back up the stairs, the whole class was waiting for her, jump ropes in hand. They all offered smiles of encouragement. She even got a few "good jobs". When she glanced at herself in the mirror, she could see how red and blotchy her face was. It wasn't the exertion. It was obvious that she had been crying. Violet took the rope Faye had grabbed for her. She fought tears for the rest of the class, but a few managed to trickle out, mixing with the sweat that poured down her face.

*

It was tempting to fall flat on the floor once Margaret called their final time, but Violet had to get out of there. She'd held up the whole class five separate times and actually cried in front of a group of skinny, in-shape strangers, as she tried to remember the proper way to get both feet over a jump rope. She couldn't look at Faye as she wiped off her face and shoved her hand towel into her canvas tote bag. Faye knew Violet wasn't ready for this, but she'd convinced to her to come anyway.

I get it, Violet thought. *You proved your point. You take care of yourself. I don't. You can handle the free production food in moderation. I can't.*

"You ready?" Faye asked. Violet simply nodded but, just as she started to follow Faye out the door, Muscle-Bound Margaret, the self-worth eater, called her name.

"Hey, Violet! Hold on one sec."

Great. Now a pep talk. "I'll meet you down at the car," she told Faye, who took the hint and promptly disappeared out the door, leaving Violet alone with the trainer.

Margaret led her over to the counter at the front of the gym and, for the first time in over an hour, the woman seemed to unclench. She gave Violet a normal smile, full of understanding and lacking false encouragement. "This class isn't for you."

Or not. "Uh, thanks?"

"Sorry, love. I didn't mean for you to take it that way. I'm supposed to tell you that you did awesome and you should come back, 'cause money and word of mouth, etcetera, but you need to scale it back. When was the last time you worked out?"

Violet felt like crying again. "Four months ago."

"And you don't like the yelling either, do you?"

"I fucking hate it, but I need something. I really do want to lose weight."

"That's great, but sometimes you need to start slowly. Your friend's been to my class seven or eight times. Yeah, there's a first time for everyone, but not everyone needs to start in the same place."

Violet swallowed and fought back sudden tears of anger. Was she that far gone that a trainer was telling her she was a lost cause? She kept her mouth shut, confident that she would never set foot in Pinks Women's Fitness ever again. Faye could drag someone else along to suffer through the humiliation.

"I know this guy. Grant. He's a great personal trainer. He has a reputation of being a complete softy, but he gets results."

Despite the fact that Violet kinda wanted to kick Margaret in her muscular shin, the idea of working with a *nice* trainer, someone who would be patient with her, one on one, sounded pretty appealing. It would also be harder for her to be jealous of a guy's body. She wouldn't spend their time together constantly comparing her breasts or her ass to his.

"That might be cool," she finally said.

"I'm going to see him later today actually. You signed in with your info, right?" Margaret looked down at the very sign-in sheet by her elbow. There was Violet's name, right above Faye's. They'd been the first to arrive.

"Yeah." Violet pointed to her name, neatly printed in blue ink. She figured if the staff at Pinks flooded her inbox with class schedules and protein shake promotions, she'd force herself to come back. That was before the second two hundred meter run.

"So you don't chicken out, I'll have him call you. I don't want you to give up, but you will if you're not matched with some class or some trainer who's right for you."

"You're right. Thanks."

After a quick goodbye, Violet left the gym, feeling a little less hostile toward Margaret. But she still had to ride back to Culver City with Faye, who was a little too perky for Violet's liking when she got into the car. Faye didn't even ask what Margaret wanted. She knew. Pat the fat girl on the back. Keep her spirits high.

"We still on for lunch?" Faye asked.

Violet was starving, but she shook her head. "I don't think so. Can you drop me off? I really want to shower and take a nap." Faye looked disappointed, but she didn't argue as she pulled her car out onto Santa Monica. Violet was quiet the whole way back to her apartment, while Faye gabbed cheerfully, refusing to acknowledge that she may have fucked up.

When they stopped in front of her place, Violet came to the conclusion that one workout shouldn't be the end of their friendship. She just needed a little space and some time to feel like herself again.

"Let's get lunch tomorrow and go see a movie or something," she suggested.

"Sure. Let's do it. And I'm sorry. I didn't think it would be that bad. I didn't want you to cry."

"I know," Violet replied. "I just need a few." Faye smiled then offered Violet her signature air kiss before Violet hopped out of the car. By the time she made it upstairs, Violet wasn't upset anymore. Just sweaty and exhausted, and fixated on inhaling everything in her fridge.

✱

After Grant finished his second Beach Bootcamp class of the day, he headed back to Melrose Fitness, where he found Australian Pump Fit champ, Margaret White, waiting for him outside the gym doors.

"Well, if it isn't my favorite Aussie. G'day, Marge."

Margaret laughed, throwing back her head and showing off her chiseled chin.

"It's scary how good you are at that accent. You sound just like my brother."

Grant kept on with the thick impression a moment longer. "Just one of my many talents. What can I do ya for?" He held the front door open, then nodded toward the back office as he kept walking. Margaret followed. Armando was still on the floor, in room two, doing a private yoga session with two of his clients from Beverly Hills, so he and Margaret had the small space, cluttered with Melrose Fitness swag and protein bars, to themselves.

Margaret plopped down into the free chair while Grant dug through his bag for a towel and a clean shirt. He had to shower before his next session.

He looked over his shoulder at Margaret. "What's up?"

"I think I have a new client for you."

"Oh yeah? Tell me about her." He flashed his friend a wicked smile.

"Such a bastard. Her name's Violet Ryan. Her friend brought her into the Pump Fit class I do over at Pinks." Grant grunted as he stripped off his shirt. Pinks provided a female-only fitness environment just a few miles up the road. They were on to something for sure, but intense workouts like Pump Fit weren't for everyone.

"Let me guess. She couldn't finish the class?"

"She finished, but there were a lot of tears. I talked to her after. She wants to get in shape, but she needs someone softer. You know how screaming gives me a hard on."

"I do. Give me her info and I'll see what I can do. You think she's ready?"

"Is anyone ready for *the* Grant Gibson?" Margaret asked, with a smile.

"You have a point."

"I think she's ready. She was just overwhelmed. You've got that soft touch she might need." Grant had no witty response for that. It was part of his reputation. He was a bit of bastard otherwise, but when it came to his clients he prided himself on being able to provide them with a relaxed, pressure-free environment where they could reach their health and fitness goals.

Margaret slipped him a piece of paper with Violet's name and phone number. "Be nice, but not too nice."

"But nice is all I know."

"Right. I'll see you later. I have some kickin' and punchin' to do." Margaret left to join Keira's four-thirty kick boxing class, but not without slugging Grant a solid one in the shoulder. Girl had an arm.

Once he was alone, per standard operating procedure with all referrals, Grant pulled out his laptop and started searching for information on Violet Ryan. It was one thing, meeting a walk-in face-to-face for the first time, but if someone was handed off to him, or Armando, or anyone else on his staff, he liked to be prepared. You'd be amazed what you could discover from someone's Twitter feed or their Facebook page. Picture after picture of high calorie meals littered Instagram and Tumblr. Eating habits, drinking habits, sedentary habits.

Are they posting nonsense in the middle of the night, then complaining about having to be at work first thing in the morning, then having the balls to say they have no time to work out? Are they venting about something going on at work or with family or a significant other? Are they having a hard time finding that special someone? All of these things played into a person's health, whether they wanted to acknowledge it or not, and it was his job to get to the bottom of it all. That's how he kept clients and saw them through to their goals. His blessing and his curse. He could read people. Make them comfortable enough to trust him to help them turn their lives around. He'd built a business to be proud of but, man, was he bored.

It didn't take long for him to find Violet Ryan, but from Margaret's brief description of her and the way she'd crumbled in a class, Grant was surprised by what he found. She was a TV producer, with credits stacked in the online television and movie database. All the producers he knew were cutthroat and coldblooded. He couldn't imagine any of them bursting into tears in front of a group of people.

He clicked through to her Facebook page and suddenly things slid into place. Violet Ryan, Associate Producer with the Food Channel, was pretty plump. It wasn't a judgment, just a fact. Same as the fact that she was a stunningly gorgeous Asian woman. She smiled in her tiny profile picture, full pink lips below an adorable button nose that was spattered with freckles. She had big brown eyes behind red-framed glasses. Her long, thick hair was doing that black-to-blond thing a lot of women were styling these days.

She managed to be hot and cute and sexy all at the same time.

He looked at her picture again. Well, stared was more like it. He would call her. A client was a client. He'd do what he could to help her out, but other parts of his brain were churning, parts that had been quiet and still for several months now.

He'd been out of the scene for a while. Life as a sexual Dominant had its perks and just as many pitfalls. He'd taken a break, taken some time to pull himself back together, but in the back of his mind he knew he wasn't out of the game forever. The game had consumed too much of his life for him to really let go.

On the flipside, Grant wasn't opposed to mixing his primary business with pleasure. He'd slept with clients before and he was sure he'd do it again. Armando did it all the fucking the time. The two of them had met at a pseudo-bondage party, grew close over their interest in kink and their obsessive dedication to working out, and eventually decided to go into business together. They'd both trained submissives and the occasional Mistress when things got a little routine. They'd both played inside and outside of the gym but lately, at least for Grant, things had been a little slow, even if it was by choice.

Everything had been slow. The classes and training sessions had grown routine, even with the occasional new client thrown into the mix. He had no woman to call his own. His family was three thousand miles away and more than happy with his simple monthly call home. He was bored and, even though it would take a lot for him to admit it openly, outside of this gym he was lonely. He had his friends, his pets, and his co-workers, but not much else. He didn't know when, but at some point something needed to change. He needed a change.

He continued clicking through picture after picture of Violet's smiling face, until Armando came through the office door. An hour of yoga and he hadn't broken a sweat.

"What's up, man?" Armando rummaged through his own things until he produced his cell phone.

"Nothing," Grant said. "Well, new client shit, but nothing."

Armando leaned over the desk and got a better look at Grant's computer screen. "This her?"

"Yeah."

"She's cute, and I assume she can afford you. What's the problem?" Armando asked, his interest in the conversation already waning. He had another class to teach in forty minutes. So did Grant, but his buddy was already thinking about the next group of clients. Grant was stuck on Violet Ryan and her innocent freckles.

"I'm thinking about dusting off the D/s file."

Armando froze in his tracks, then pivoted around to face Grant.

"I know. It's risky," Grant said.

"It's not risky, it's—"

"Risky."

"No, you can handle it. I know you can. I just didn't know you were ready. Is Ariana that far from your head? She was a dick, but I figured you learned something from that."

"She wasn't a dick."

"She stole your credit cards and tried to steal Max when you broke up with her."

It had been six months since he ended things with his client-turned-submissive. His credit rating and his dog were still trying to recover. It wasn't that he'd slept with her, it was that he'd trusted her more than he should. He was looking for love and she was looking for someone to bleed dry. "You're right, she was a dick, but I think it might be time."

"Good luck, man." Armando looked at the screen again, his expression one of genuine approval. "Could be fun."

Grant clicked through her pictures one more time. Before his imagination got the best of him, he grabbed his cellphone and dialed Violet Ryan's number.

CPSIA information can be obtained
at www.ICGtesting.com
Printed in the USA
LVOW11s1645151217
559880LV00001B/39/P